SECRET OF THE
UNSEEN TREASURE

Trixie
Belden

Your TRIXIE BELDEN Library

Trixie Belden and the
SECRET OF THE
UNSEEN TREASURE

BY KATHRYN KENNY

Cover by Jack Wacker

GOLDEN PRESS
Western Publishing Company, Inc.
Racine, Wisconsin

CONTENTS

SECRET OF THE UNSEEN TREASURE

Stranger in the Garden • 1

T<small>RIXIE</small> B<small>ELDEN</small> bounced into the kitchen. Her blue eyes sparkled, and her sandy curls lifted as though they shared her excitement.

"Oh, Moms, I feel so free!" she said to Mrs. Belden, who was carefully removing cake layers from the oven to cooling racks. "Just think! School is out. I'm *free* for the whole summer. Nothing to do except—"

"Except," her mother interposed, glancing over her shoulder, "to keep your room clean, do your chores around the house and in the garden, and take care of Bobby now and then. Unless, of course, you plan to give up your five dollars a week allowance."

"Oh, Moms." Trixie tried to hide the dismay in her voice. "I didn't mean I wouldn't do all those things!"

"Indubitably not," scoffed Mart Belden. Eleven months older than Trixie, he detested being mistaken for her twin. He liked to use big words, especially to tease Trixie. "You were just wishing you could eschew those responsibilities during your summer hiatus."

"I was not!" Trixie retorted.

In the doorway, seventeen-year-old Brian Belden combed fingers through his dark, wavy hair and winked at his mother. "I suggest they both be kept out of trouble by enrolling them in summer school." He grinned at their mother's suddenly thoughtful expression. "Meanwhile, I'll convey their apologies to Honey for not coming over to help exercise the Wheelers' horses."

Honey Wheeler was Trixie's best friend. She

14

lived at the Manor House on the gently sloping hillside just west of the Beldens' modest Crab-apple Farm. The Wheelers were one of the wealthiest families in the town of Sleepyside-on-the-Hudson, just north of New York City. They maintained a stable of fine horses that needed more exercise than the older members of the Wheeler household had time to give them. Riding was a frequent pastime for the Bob-Whites of the Glen, the club formed by Trixie and her friends.

The B.W.G.'s had planned to start off their school vacation with a horseback ride this after-noon. Now Trixie was worried about her moth-er's reminder of chores.

"Moms . . ." she began, pleading.

Six-year-old Bobby interrupted. "You prom-ised to take me and Reddy for a walk." He called to the Beldens' big Irish setter, who was pawing at the screen door. "Trixie and me will be right out, Reddy."

"Bobby," Mrs. Belden said kindly, "I thought we agreed we wouldn't interfere with Trixie's plans for this afternoon. Anyway, I'll need your help to put the icing on the cake and lick the bowl clean."

"Moms!" Trixie exclaimed. "Do you really mean it? I can go? You won't be mad?"

"I know you'll attend to your chores sooner or later."

"Undoubtedly later," Mart remarked.

"Oh, go stick your head in a dictionary and close it hard," Trixie retorted. She hugged her mother. "I promise I'll do them real soon. Thanks, Moms, for being so kind and understanding."

"I remember how it feels when school lets out for the summer," said Mrs. Belden, laughing. "Believe it or not, I was your age once upon a time."

Bobby looked bewildered. "Was Trixie *your* baby-sitter, too?"

"No, Bobby. Mrs. Elliot was."

"Mrs. Elliot?" Trixie asked. "I always thought your sitter's name was Ethel Rogers."

"That was her name," Mrs. Belden said, "before she married Sam Elliot, a widower with a teen-age son."

Trixie frowned. "Is Max Elliot her stepson? He's been working for her since early in the spring."

"Sure he is," said Mart. "He ran away from home just before Mr. Elliot died five years ago. Now he's back."

"Mart," Mrs. Belden chided, "you don't make that sound very nice."

"Well, he did run away," Mart said. "He probably thought he couldn't get anywhere by raising flowers and vegetables with his father. I wonder what made him decide to come back here now."

"Maybe he found out life's not so easy in the city either," Mrs. Belden said. "Anyway, it's nice that Ethel Elliot has his help. She's barely been able to hold on to the place with just Social Security payments and the produce she's been able to raise and sell. Maybe now she'll have time to attend garden club meetings again and start winning prizes with her flowers." Mrs. Belden looked up at Trixie. "Have you changed your mind about going riding?"

"Don't count on it," Brian said with a laugh.

"Well, be careful," their mother advised. "Stay out of trouble."

"You heard what she said," Mart reminded Trixie as they walked the short distance to Manor House. "Stay out of trouble."

"That's impossible with you around," Trixie replied loftily.

"You know what I mean," Mart persisted. "Just don't go looking for a mystery to keep everyone in a dither all summer."

Brian pushed in so he could walk between them. "Relax, you two," he said diplomatically.

"He's just pretending," Trixie declared to Brian. "He really *enjoys* helping when Honey and I find a mystery."

Trixie and Honey were always looking for a mystery that needed solving. In fact, they had hopes of someday running their own detective agency.

"Simply a matter of predilection—or, rather, lack of choice," Mart remarked.

Their arrival at Manor House was announced noisily by Jim's springer spaniel, Patch.

"Hi, Patch," said Trixie, stooping to scratch

18

behind his ears. "Where's Honey?"

"Changing clothes," replied a voice from somewhere behind Trixie.

Trixie didn't turn. She knelt and raised her voice in mock surprise. "Why, Patch! You sound just like Miss Trask." Miss Trask was manager of the Wheeler household. "When did you learn to talk?"

"Arf! Arf!" Miss Trask replied. "I taught him."

"Arf! Arf!" Patch joined in.

"Now he's teaching you," Trixie said, chuckling. Turning, she faced Miss Trask, as trim-looking as ever in a light blue summer suit and small straw hat with matching band. As usual, Miss Trask wore sensible, serviceable, sturdy-looking oxfords.

"How nice you look!" Trixie exclaimed.

Mart nodded, then glanced disparagingly at his sister. "Why don't you try emulating her sometime? Look at you: scuffed shoes, faded jeans, a blouse that is—"

Miss Trask interrupted: "—that is just right for a casual afternoon ride." She sighed. "I wish

I could go along, but I have to go into town instead."

"Oh, good!" Trixie said without thinking. "I mean, that's awful. I mean, I'm sorry. I didn't want to sound like—"

"No apologies needed." Miss Trask smiled. "You won't be interfering with my plans by riding Susie."

"That's what I meant to say," Trixie explained lamely.

"Even if I didn't have to go to town," Miss Trask said understandingly, "I wouldn't consider spoiling your plans for today. I know how it feels when school lets out for the summer. Believe me, it's a relief for the teachers, too!"

Miss Trask strolled with them toward the stable. As they passed the garage, Brian moved ahead eagerly. Earlier in the day, he had left his beat-up car to be tuned by Tom Delanoy, the Wheelers' chauffeur.

"How's it running, Tom?"

Tom rolled his twinkling blue eyes. "It would have been simpler if you hadn't messed around with it first."

"Sometimes engines are better off without my help," Brian agreed.

"And yet," Tom said with a grin, "you plan to become a doctor and take care of human engines."

"You just lost a patient, doc." It was Dan Mangan, coming out of the garage, who had spoken. A few years ago, Dan had been living in the city and headed for trouble. His uncle, Regan, the Wheelers' horse trainer, had brought him to Sleepyside, and the B.W.G.'s had helped to get him back on the right track. Now he lived with Mr. Maypenny, the gamekeeper for the Wheeler estate.

"Brian will be a fine doctor," Tom corrected. "When I accidentally gashed my arm, he did a good job of first aid. There wasn't anything left for Dr. Gregory to do except give me a tetanus shot."

"Hi, everybody!" Honey Wheeler came running from the house. She was the same age as Trixie, but taller and slimmer. She had hazel eyes and golden brown hair that earned her the nickname Honey. She waved an envelope.

21

"Mother asked if we would ride to Mrs. Elliot's and drop this off. It's a thank-you note for the flowers she provided for Mother's luncheon yesterday."

"And also a check for the flowers," Miss Trask reminded her. "So be careful not to lose it. Mrs. Elliot needs any help she can get."

Another "Hi!" sounded, more subdued than Honey's. Diana Lynch, the quietest member of the B.W.G.'s, always let her large violet eyes express what her voice didn't. Her long, blue-black hair made a shining frame for her pretty face.

"All ready and accounted for—except Jim," said Trixie.

"He's already in the stable," Dan told her. "But you'll have to count me out for now. I've got to help Mr. Maypenny finish putting out salt blocks for the deer, and then I have to do some errands in town. I'll see you guys and gals later!"

"Let's get going," said Trixie, starting down the sloping drive bordered by pink and red hollyhocks.

Honey hurried past her. "Last one to the stable can groom Lady for me!"

Everyone ran, shouting and laughing.

Bill Regan, the horse trainer, appeared in the wide stable doorway. He hunched his broad shoulders and raised his hands to his red head in mock dismay.

"Oh, is this going to be an afternoon to survive!" he said. "Frisky horses getting out for the first time in days—and frisky kids just out of school."

"Regan," Trixie apologized, "we haven't had time to exercise the horses. We all had to study for final exams. If we hadn't passed, we'd be in school all summer. Then you *would* have a problem getting the horses exercised!"

"All right, all right." Regan grinned. "They're all groomed and waiting." He forced a stern expression on his pleasant face. "But from now on, through the summer, you kids do the grooming and take care of the tack. Now, get 'em out and saddle up. Honey, mind how Lady blows herself up when you take up the girth."

"I won't forget," Honey replied, recalling

how the saddle had once slipped to the side, comically spilling her off the dapple-gray mare.

Trixie entered the stable, savoring the smells of oats, bran, polished leather, and horses. As she opened a box stall, she reached into the pocket of her jeans for a carrot.

"Hi, Susie. Remember me?" Trixie spoke softly to Miss Trask's beautiful little black mare. The horse's coat gleamed like dark satin after Regan's currycombing and brushing. Velvety lips gently accepted the carrot from Trixie's palm. Then, crunching away contentedly, the mare made no fuss about the bridle being slipped on.

Out in the gangway, there was an excited tattoo of hooves. Trixie saw that it was Jupiter, Mr. Wheeler's black stallion. No one but Mr. Wheeler, Regan, and Jim Frayne could manage him. Jim, who firmly held Jupiter now, had been rescued from a very cruel stepfather by Honey's parents, who had adopted him. Jim had red hair like Mr. Wheeler and had become like a real son to his foster parents and a real brother to Honey.

"All right, Jupe, take it easy," Jim said sooth-ingly, holding close to the bit. "Just a minute and we'll be ready to go."

Regan spoke quietly. "Don't let him have his head right off, Jim. Wait until he knows *you're* the boss, not him. That goes for all of you. Don't let your mounts take command."

The frisky horses wanted to run, but Trixie and the others held them to a walk for a quar-ter of a mile. Bees hummed, birds sang, and the sweet scent of honeysuckle and the tang of wild huckleberries filled the air.

Jim, leading the way on Jupe, turned off Glen Road onto a trail into the hills. "Anyone ready to canter?" he called back.

"The horses are," Trixie replied. "And so are we!"

Jupe wanted to go all out on the trail, but Jim remained in control, setting the pace at a steady canter. Trixie's mare Susie drummed after them, with Honey right alongside on the dapple-gray Lady. The others were close be-hind.

When they reached the crest of a long, steady

slope, Jim reined in his mount. "That ought to take some of the edge off them," he said, breathing hard.

"That was fun!" Trixie exclaimed.

Di, the quiet one, nodded and smiled.

"As soon as they get their wind back," Mart suggested, "let's do it again."

"Whoa," Brian cautioned. "Regan won't like it if we bring them back overheated."

While they gave the horses a breather, Trixie gazed down into a picturesque, secluded little valley. Mrs. Elliot's cottage nestled there, a white bungalow surrounded by flowers of all colors, like a pearl amid bright gems. Beyond the flowers, neat rows of vegetables formed a small truck garden. A larger area toward the mouth of the valley was lush with corn. In the dark green center of the cornfield, a man leaned on a hoe.

"That must be Max," said Honey.

"Working hard, isn't he?" Mart gibed.

"Just like when you're supposed to be helping me hoe the garden at home," retorted Trixie quickly.

"Maybe he *is* working," Mart replied. "Testing out my theory."

"What theory?" Honey inquired.

"Well," Mart explained, "kind words are supposed to make flowers and other desirable verdure burgeon. So unkind words should make weeds atrophy and die. Right?"

"There's only one answer to that," Brian commented. "Hoe-hoe-hoe!"

"Oh!" Jim winced. "That's awful."

Trixie was only half listening to the banter. Her eye had detected some movement near the hothouse and potting shed behind the cottage. She couldn't quite make out what it was—maybe Mrs. Elliot doing some gardening there. But then a man moved into Trixie's view. He had a can in his hand and seemed to be watering plants close to the buildings. He was dressed in a suit and tie.

"Who's *that* man?" Trixie asked, pointing at the stranger.

"Whoever he is," Honey observed, "he certainly isn't dressed for gardening!"

"And he's sure sloppy about watering," Mart

27

said. "He's getting more on the building than on the plants."

"That's strange," Jim added. "He's using a red can, like the kind you use to carry gas!"

Those words were taken right out of Trixie's mouth.

"Honey! Mart! Di!" she shouted. "Quick! Ride down to the cornfield. Tell Max!"

The three horses lunged down the hill toward the cornfield. Jim was already charging Jupe toward the potting shed. Trixie urged Susie into pursuit. Brian galloped alongside. "Not too fast downhill," he warned.

"That man is going to set fire to Mrs. Elliot's property!"

"We're not sure of that," Brian shouted. "He could be an exterminator or something like that."

Trixie shook her head emphatically. "Not dressed like that!"

Hooves drummed and clattered down the hill. Through an opening in the trees near the bottom, Trixie glimpsed the man looking over his shoulder at them. She yelled and pointed in his direction to let him know he'd been spotted.

Then they were on the floor of the little valley. Jupe leaped over a small brook, and his hooves gouged the earth on the drive alongside Mrs. Elliot's cottage. Brian swerved Starlight to the right in pursuit. Trixie followed on Susie. She didn't rein in until she swung around a corner of the barn and almost collided with the other horses. Jim was already on foot, running toward the abandoned red can, lying on its side and gurgling pungent gasoline. He set the can upright and turned quickly to scan the area around the potting shed. There was no sign of fire.

"We scared him off," Jim said.

Then they heard a car roar off down the lane, concealed by trees and bushes.

"What on earth is going on here?" Mrs. Elliot, wiping her hands on a dish towel, appeared beside Trixie. She sounded as if she didn't know whether to be angry or worried at the way the young people had come charging onto her property. Then she smelled the gasoline, and her face twisted with fear.

"What's going on here?" she repeated in a trembling voice.

Trixie shook her head. "That's what we'd like to know."

Clues—and More Mystery · 2

MRS. ELLIOT was lean and strong from years of gardening. Her eyes, as blue as delphiniums, peered through thick glasses. Her deeply tanned face was framed by short, curly gray hair. At the moment, her cheeks were flushed with fear.

"Mrs. Elliot," Trixie said quickly, "we saw a man try to set fire to your shed."

Jim pointed to the gasoline can. "He was pouring gasoline on the side of the building.

Fortunately, we scared him off before he did any real harm."

Mrs. Elliot looked at the climbing clematis along the wall of the shed. The leaves, wet with gasoline, were already wilting.

"He *has* done real harm. Gasoline will kill the plants. Nothing will grow in that soil for years." She looked bewildered. "But if he'd burned down my potting shed. . . ."

"Why would anyone do that?" Trixie asked, as Honey, Mart, and Di came riding up to the shed.

"I've no idea. I just can't believe it," Mrs. Elliot sighed.

"Maybe an arsonist," Mart said. "A nut."

"I don't think so," Trixie declared.

"Why?" Mart demanded.

"I—I don't know," she admitted. "I just have a feeling. . . ."

"Whatever the reason," Jim said seriously, "I'm glad we scared him off before he lit a match. A fire might have spread to the barn and caused a lot of damage."

Mrs. Elliot's eyes widened as she imagined

the possible destruction. "That would be the end of my business," she said. "Of course, it's not the way it was when my husband was alive. Then we sold large volumes of flowers and produce. Now . . . well, there's one flower shop in White Plains that takes some blossoms. Most people around here have their own gardens, so I sell only special arrangements occasionally. I need that income to eke out what Social Security doesn't cover."

"That reminds me," Honey said, taking the envelope from the pocket of her jeans. "Mother asked me to give this to you."

"Thank you." Mrs. Elliot put a hand to her forehead and looked at the concerned faces of the group of youngsters. "And thank you for what you all did."

Max Elliot came running past the cottage. His dark eyes flashed, and there was an angry glow under the tan of his unshaven cheeks. "Did he get away?"

"Yes," Trixie answered. "I guess that's my fault. I yelled at him as we rode down the hill."

"It's a good thing you did," Jim reassured

her. "If you hadn't, he would have started the fire. By the time the fire department could get out here from Sleepyside. . . ."

Max Elliot turned to Trixie. "Did any of you get a good look at him?"

"Only from a distance," Trixie said.

"I almost saw him," Di said. "After we rode to the cornfield to tell Max, I saw a car racing down the lane on the other side."

"What kind of car?" Jim asked.

"I couldn't see that much of it—only the top."

"What color was it?" Brian asked.

Di shook her head. "The sun was too bright, reflecting in my eyes. All I saw was the glare."

Max looked at his stepmother. "Guess we'll never know." He stepped toward the gasoline can.

"Don't touch it!" Trixie cried out. "We should call Sergeant Molinson. There may be fingerprints."

"Of course there will," Max said. "Mine. This is my gasoline can. Our can," he corrected himself, glancing at Mrs. Elliot. "It's one we keep in the pickup."

"Are you sure?" Trixie asked.

He pointed to a metallic spot where the red paint had been chipped away. "It's ours," he said dourly.

"Well," Mart commented, "that shoots down what I said. An arsonist would probably have brought his own gasoline."

Trixie moved determinedly to the gasoline can. "Let's call Sergeant Molinson," she suggested to Mrs. Elliot.

Ten minutes later, the police car came up the Elliot lane. Sergeant Molinson got out and frowned at the B.W.G.'s, particularly Trixie. "What are you kids involved in now?"

"We're witnesses," Trixie replied.

Mrs. Elliot spoke to the sergeant. "Someone tried to set a fire here. These young people saw the attempt and prevented it."

Molinson sighed. "All right, tell me about it."

Trixie, Honey, and Jim all started to talk at once.

"One at a time!" Molinson snapped.

Honey and Jim looked at Trixie. Ignoring

her, Molinson gestured to Jim. "You first. Then the others, *if* I think it's necessary."

Jim told how, as they were resting the horses on the hill, they had seen the man pouring gasoline around the shed.

"How could you tell from up there that it was gasoline?" Molinson inquired.

"We couldn't for sure, of course," Jim replied. "But it was a red can—that one over there —and he was wearing a suit, not dressed for gardening. So we assumed—"

"Assumed," Molinson repeated.

"We assumed correctly!" Trixie declared. "It *was* gasoline. And the man's fingerprints will be on that can."

"He wasn't wearing gloves?" Molinson queried sharply.

Trixie felt deflated. She hadn't looked at the man's hands. Neither had the other B.W.G.'s.

"I thought so," Molinson remarked.

"But you'll still check that can?" Trixie asked timidly.

"Of course," Molinson replied. "And I'll probably find all *your* prints on it."

"Just Jim's and Max's that we know of," Trixie told him.

"Good," said Molinson. "Jim and Max will have to stop by the station as soon as possible so I can take their prints. Then we'll know which ones to eliminate on the can. That's all I need from you kids." Sergeant Molinson produced a handkerchief and picked up the gas can by slipping it through the handle. He, Max, and Mrs. Elliot headed for the driveway.

Trixie caught Honey's eye, then handed Susie's reins to Mart. Honey gave Lady's reins to Brian.

"Now what are you up to?" Mart murmured.

Trixie didn't reply. Instead, she led Honey through the trees to the lane where they had heard the car roar off. There they found scuffed damp earth where tires had spun as the man had fled. Trixie moved slowly in the opposite direction. She followed the faint tire tracks to a spot of flattened grass and weeds.

"He must have driven up the lane," Trixie noted, "then turned the car around before going to Mrs. Elliot's."

"That was probably so he could make a fast getaway after starting the fire," Honey reasoned. "But he had to make it faster than planned, thanks to you."

"Thanks to the B.W.G.'s," Trixie corrected her. She stepped farther off the lane to where the car had backed into the bushes and broken some of the branches and twigs. Trixie peered at the bruised bark of a maple sapling that had been scraped.

"Honey," she called. "Take a look at this."

Before Honey could join her, Sergeant Molinson spoke from behind them. "I thought I told you I didn't need you anymore."

"We've found some more evidence for you," said Trixie. She pointed to the bruised bark. "Some paint was scraped off the car. It looks like gray."

"That's a big help," Molinson grumbled. "There must be thousands of gray cars registered with the Department of Motor Vehicles. It might be a car from Connecticut, Rhode Island, New Jersey. . . ."

Trixie nodded, discouraged. "We may never

find out who would try to do such a terrible thing to Mrs. Elliot. She's such a sweet, kindly person—"

"I know," Molinson interrupted. "When one of my officers was hurt recently, she took flowers to the hospital every day and gave vegetables to his wife and children." Molinson's glance moved from Trixie to Honey and back again. "I'd like to get my hands on the creep, too." He sighed. "But with the little I've got to go on, it doesn't seem very likely."

His tone hardened as he looked at the weeds and grass flattened by tires and feet. "I hope you haven't destroyed other possible evidence here, trying to play detective. I appreciate your concern, but, as I said before, you'd better be on your way."

As she and Honey walked toward the cottage, Trixie said wryly, "I knew that friendly tone of his was too good to last."

Back at the potting shed, most of the gasoline had evaporated. Just to be safe, Jim was watering down the area with a garden hose.

Mrs. Elliot brought out a tray with a pitcher

of lemonade and a plate of chocolate chip cookies. "I don't know how I can ever thank you," she said.

"Me, too," said Max, scowling at the building. "Not that the shed would have been much of a loss. But the idea of someone trying to destroy it—"

"Is it insured?" Jim asked.

Max shook his head. "Too old and run-down," he replied.

"I couldn't afford any insurance anyway," said Mrs. Elliot. "But there are tools stored in there. And I need the hothouse on the side for some of my plants, like hyacinths and lilies for Easter, and poinsettias for Christmas."

"Your flowers are beautiful, Mrs. Elliot," said Trixie, looking around. "I wish I had a green thumb like you and Max."

Max snorted. "I can't grow a thing. All I'm good for is knocking down weeds. And I'd better get after them if we're going to have any corn to sell." He moved away toward the cornfield.

Mrs. Elliot gazed after him. "Max still has

too much of the city in him," she murmured. "Everything happens so fast there. But with growing things, you have to learn to wait, to be patient."

"I guess I'm not very patient," Trixie admitted. "I tried planting sweet peas this spring, but I gave up and quit watering them before they blossomed."

"Let me give you a bouquet of mine," Mrs. Elliot said. Ignoring Trixie's protests, she led the way through the garden. "You mustn't wait until too late in the spring to plant sweet peas, Trixie. You should dig a deep trench in good loamy soil, well fertilized. Soak the seeds overnight before planting them, then keep the soil moist."

"I'll remember what you said next time," Trixie said. "But the plants kept falling down."

"That's natural for them," Mrs. Elliot explained. "It's called 'stooping.' They'll grow more roots and climbers. Just be sure they have something to climb on. Chicken wire is fine, or a trellis, or string."

Trixie gasped at the sight of a huge pillar of

colorful sweet peas. Then she spotted the opened frame of an old umbrella, hanging from the beam of the arbor facing the sun. From each umbrella rib, stout twine hung to the ground for the sweet peas to climb on.

"What a neat idea!" Trixie exclaimed.

"It does create a pleasing effect, doesn't it?" Mrs. Elliot said. She smiled and explained sheepishly, "I needed something for them to climb on. I didn't have any chicken wire and couldn't afford to buy any. I found this old umbrella frame that I'd never gotten around to having re-covered. It just goes to show what you can get by with if you really put your mind to it."

"I think it's beautiful," Trixie said. Her eyes danced from color to color: lavender, pink, blue, red, white, and yellow. "So many colors! And the stems are so big—not like my scrawny plants at all."

"That comes from good feeding and watering," said Mrs. Elliot. She began snipping and collecting a bouquet.

"Oh, don't cut too many," Trixie protested.

Mrs. Elliot shook her head. "If the blossoms aren't taken off, the vines will go to seed instead of creating more blooms."

Trixie frowned at the size of the bouquet. "You shouldn't *give* so many away."

"Why not? Flowers are for sharing with others. And," Mrs. Elliot sighed, "they don't sell the way they used to."

"But they should," Trixie said. "They're so beautiful."

Mrs. Elliot handed Trixie a lovely bouquet. "It's warm today, so I'll wrap these cut ends in some damp moss to keep the flowers fresh."

Riding back to Manor House, Trixie raised the bouquet to smell the sweet scent.

Honey was watching her. "You're sniffing more than flowers," she said.

Trixie nodded absently. "There's a lot about this afternoon I just can't believe."

"You mean you can't believe that school is out?" Honey asked.

Trixie gave her a scowl.

Honey nodded. "I know. It's Mrs. Elliot. I

43

can't believe it either, that someone would want to destroy her property."

Trixie urged Susie ahead to pace alongside Jim on Jupe. "When you go down to the police station to let Sergeant Molinson take your fingerprints, I'd like to go with you."

Jim grinned. "I'll enjoy your company, but he won't."

Mart overheard. "Now what are you concocting, sister?"

"Some way to help Mrs. Elliot. And," Trixie added quickly to forestall any more questions, "among other things, when her corn is ready, I think we should buy some and have a corn roast."

The B.W.G.'s all agreed.

When they arrived at Manor House, Regan eyed the horses. "Good," he commented. "They're not overheated or winded. Give them a rubdown, then water and feed them. How was Mrs. Elliot?"

Regan's big hands clenched when he heard about the arson attempt.

Dan, back from town, stood to one side, listening quietly and frowning. "Would you recognize the man if you saw him again?" he asked.

The B.W.G.'s explained that they'd only seen the man from a distance.

"But we did find some other clues," Trixie said.

Dan's frown deepened. "I think you should leave this to Sergeant Molinson."

"Why?" Trixie asked.

Dan shrugged. "I just think that you should. Arson is serious business. Dangerous."

"Dan's right," Regan agreed. "Any guy who'd want to set fire to a struggling widow's property has got to be really sick. It's a good thing that *he* didn't get a better look at you kids. So keep out of it. Don't play with fire!"

The B.W.G.'s were silent as they groomed the horses and cleaned the tack. When Brian and Mart were ready to leave for home, Trixie lingered behind.

"Tell Moms I'm going to ride into Sleepyside with Jim," she said.

"My earlier testimony has been corroborated," Mart commented. "She'll get around to her chores sooner or later—emphasis on later."

Trixie thrust the bouquet at him. "Stick your nose in this. Maybe it'll sweeten your thoughts. Give it to Moms."

"Peace offering?" Mart asked mockingly.

Trixie sneered. "Jim will drop me off at home as soon as he's through at the police station."

On the two-mile drive into town, Jim was thoughtful. While waiting for a stoplight to change, he turned to Trixie. "What Regan said really kind of scares me," he admitted. "If that guy recognized any of us and found out where we live. . . ."

Trixie shuddered. "Gleeps! He might try starting another fire. That's all the more reason for us to do anything we can to see that he's captured."

"I don't know what more we can do," Jim said, turning his eyes to the road as the light changed. "We've already told Sergeant Molinson everything we saw."

In the Sleepyside police station, Trixie remained silent. Sergeant Molinson's frown at her appearance was all the warning she needed. She stood to one side, watching, as the fingerprints of Jim's right hand were taken. Then Jim showed Sergeant Molinson where he had grasped the gas can when he had turned it upright.

The telephone on Molinson's desk rang. He answered and, after a brief conversation, began writing a series of numbers on a note pad.

Trixie turned to a cork bulletin board and began scanning the various cards and papers tacked on it. There were hints about bicycle safety. A small holder contained stickers with emergency numbers for police, fire, and ambulance, to be placed on telephones. A large color poster illustrated various kinds of harmful drugs, how they were used and what their effects were.

Molinson hung up the phone and spoke to one of his officers. "That was the local Social Security office. Here's a list of numbers of the checks that were stolen from the rural postal route on Glen Road. The office is sending out warning bulletins to all area banks. I don't think we'll see the checks around here, but make some copies of this list and get them to Lytell's store on Glen Road."

Trixie broke her silence. "Did you say the Glen Road postal route? That would include Mrs. Elliot, wouldn't it? Was her check stolen, too?"

Molinson scowled. "You're right up-to-date, aren't you? The checks were stolen ten days ago. The names of people who didn't receive their Social Security checks were in last week's paper."

Trixie reddened and spoke to Jim, who was wiping his hand on a paper towel. "I'll meet you at the car."

She hurried out of the police station and down the street to the office of the *Sleepyside Sun*. At a table in the lobby, she opened the large binder containing recent back issues of the paper. Trixie had been too busy lately with school and other activities to bother reading the newspapers delivered to Crabapple Farm. Anyway, the New York City paper was usually filled only with politics, problems of foreign countries, and big-city crime. And the *Sleepy-side Sun* had mostly news she didn't care about, either: "Mrs. Smith entertained Mrs. Jones, Mrs. Brown, and Mrs. Anderson for luncheon and bridge on Tuesday." The following week, Mrs. Jones's name would be first, because the luncheon had been at her home. Trixie seldom looked at the paper unless she expected an item about some activity in which she or her friends had participated. Remembering Molinson's scowl, Trixie vowed that she would keep more "up-to-date."

Now she scanned the story in last week's paper about the stolen checks. Mrs. Elliot's name was not on the list of people whose checks had been stolen.

Trixie called to the man sitting at a desk behind the counter. "Is this a complete list of the people who had their Social Security checks stolen?"

The man looked up. "Everyone who reported that they hadn't received their checks is listed."

Trixie left the newspaper office. If Mrs. Elliot had not received her check, why hadn't she reported it? Maybe her name had been accidentally omitted from the list in the story.

Jim, waiting beside the car, grinned as she approached. "Sergeant Molinson said that he never got rid of you that easily before."

"He's not going to discourage me," Trixie replied stiffly. "Did he say anything else about the arsonist after I left?"

Jim shook his head.

"What about fingerprints on that gas can?" Trixie asked.

"After mine were eliminated, most of the others seemed to be the same particular pattern. They're probably Max's. There were also some smudges that could have been made by gloves."

Trixie gave an exasperated sigh. "So I guess Sergeant Molinson's not going to do anything else about it."

"He didn't say," Jim said wryly.

"I wish we had time to go out to Mrs. Elliot's again," Trixie said. "There's something I'd like to ask her."

Jim hesitated, then shook his head. "From what Mart said, you'd better get home. If you get in trouble with your folks for skipping your chores, you might be grounded. Then you *would* have to leave everything up to Sergeant Molinson."

Trixie sighed again. "I guess you're right. Better get me home. Fast."

"Something Squishy" • 3

TRIXIE SUFFERED through her chores—dusting, getting Bobby washed up and into clean clothes, and helping prepare supper.

The main topic of conversation during supper was the arson attempt at Mrs. Elliot's. Peter Belden, Trixie's father, listened indulgently as Trixie insisted, "Somebody is trying to put Mrs. Elliot out of business."

"I'm afraid you're jumping to conclusions," her father said. "Mrs. Elliot doesn't make enough competition for anyone to need to 'put her out of business.' I'm inclined to think it's just a case of malicious behavior. Some vandals seem to concentrate on making the elderly their victims. They probably figure that if their vandalism is discovered, their victims will be unable to retaliate."

Mrs. Belden frowned. " 'Retaliate' isn't the word you want. 'Defend themselves' is probably what you mean."

Trixie spoke up. "Retaliate! That's it!"

"Brainstorm coming!" Mart exclaimed loudly. "Everyone batten down the hatches!"

"Mart," Mrs. Belden chided, "we don't shout at the table."

"Sorry," Mart murmured. He glanced slyly at Trixie and took a bracing grip on the edge of the table. "Proceed," he said.

"I wasn't talking to you anyway," Trixie replied. She faced her father. "Suppose Mrs. Elliot saw who stole the Social Security checks from the mailboxes on the rural route. Maybe the attempt today was a warning to keep silent about what she knows."

"That doesn't make sense," Brian observed. "The checks were stolen more than a week ago. Today's 'warning,' if it was one, was kind of late."

"Maybe there was *another* warning earlier," Trixie persisted. "One we don't know about. Maybe Mrs. Elliot was changing her mind about keeping quiet, so the arson attempt was a second, stronger warning."

"I've known Ethel Elliot most of my life," said Trixie's mother. "If she saw something illegal, she'd report it."

"Well," Trixie said slowly, "you know her better than I do. But there's one thing she didn't report. At least, from what I read in the paper, she didn't report it."

"What's that?" Mart asked. He wasn't deriding Trixie now; his curiosity had obviously been aroused.

"Mrs. Elliot didn't report the theft of her Social Security check," Trixie announced.

Peter Belden shook his head. "There's a very simple explanation for that: Her check wasn't stolen. It's not delivered to her roadside box.

54

She has Social Security mail her check directly to the bank, where it's credited to her checking account."

"Oh," said Trixie, deflated.

Peter Belden looked as though he shared her disappointment. "Of course, I wouldn't know that if I didn't work at the bank. But there you go again, Trixie, jumping to conclusions. If you and Honey were really involved someday with an investigative agency—"

"The Belden-Wheeler Detective Agency," Trixie interrupted.

Her father nodded and went on. "If you were actually doing detective work, you would have to concentrate on *facts*, not assumptions." He smiled. "Now it's a fact that I would like another helping of beans, please."

After supper, Mart came into the kitchen, where Trixie was morosely taking her turn at washing the dishes.

"I was as disappointed as you were about the supposedly stolen check," he confessed. "I thought you were really getting onto something, until Dad stuck a pin in it."

Trixie nodded. "Here," she said, extending a dish towel. "As long as you're—"

Mart quickly backed away from the towel. "My sympathy doesn't extend that far!"

"Oooooh!" Trixie chased him from the room and threw the towel after him.

In the morning, Honey telephoned. "Jim and I are going swimming in the lake this afternoon. Care to join us?"

"If I can," Trixie replied. "I'll have to find out first what Moms has planned. You know how it is."

"Yes, it's the same with Miss Trask." There was no resentment in Honey's voice, but Trixie understood what she meant. Honey's mother was nearly helpless about running the household, and she was constantly involved with social affairs or accompanying her husband on business trips. Miss Trask ran the Wheeler household.

"Mother's planning to leave for Washington with Daddy," Honey went on. "And Miss Trask thinks I ought to stay close to home. That explains the swimming this afternoon. Not that I don't enjoy swimming, but—"

"You had something else in mind?" Trixie asked.

"Mrs. Elliot," Honey replied. "I'd sure like to go back and check on her, to make sure everything is all right. But Miss Trask thinks we're trying to get too involved."

"I know what you mean," Trixie said. She told Honey about her father's remarks at supper.

Honey sighed. "They tell us they 'know how we feel' because they were young once. Then they turn right around and refuse to understand how we feel. Trixie, I just *know* that something is wrong at Mrs. Elliot's."

"How do you know?" Trixie asked.

"It's just a feeling. Has Dan been in touch with you?"

"No," said Trixie in a puzzled tone. "Why do you ask?"

"There's something very strange about his attitude."

"I noticed that yesterday when he said we

57

should stay out of it and leave everything to Sergeant Molinson," Trixie agreed. "That's not like Dan. He's usually as interested in a case as we are."

"Oh, he's interested all right," Honey declared. "But not in the usual way. Listen: I went to the stable last night to help Regan bed down the horses. Dan was there. He often drops by to visit his uncle. But I got the feeling this was more than a casual visit. Dan went out of his way to talk to me about what happened at Mrs. Elliot's."

"So?" Trixie prompted.

"He tried to make it sound offhand, but he was digging for something, if you know what I mean."

"Yep!" Trixie understood. "Just like Moms or Dad does when they're trying to get me to own up to something that they've already found out about."

Honey laughed. "Miss Trask, too. But, anyway, that's what Dan was doing. In an offhand sort of way—that didn't fool me for a minute— he wanted to know if we had seen something about that man that we would recognize again. Then he started asking about the car, still trying to sound casual. Were we sure it was a gray car? Didn't we notice anything else about it? What make was it? What color were the license plates? Things like that."

Trixie frowned. "That sounds like he had a definite car in mind."

"That's the feeling I got, too!" Honey exclaimed.

"Did you try to find out what Dan's theory is?"

"He must have known I was going to try. He suddenly remembered that he had something else to do. As he left, though, he said again that we ought to leave it to Sergeant Molinson. Miss Trask was out walking and overheard that part. I tried to tell her my feelings about Dan, but she said that he was right and that we should keep out of it."

"I know. I've heard that, too," Trixie commented dryly.

"So Miss Trask laid down the law about staying close to home." Honey sighed. "I guess we'll just have to sort of work under cover."

"Underwater, since we're going swimming," Trixie said. "See you at the lake this afternoon if it's okay with Moms."

As she hung up the phone, Trixie saw her mother in the doorway.

"The vegetables are waiting to see you do something about the weeds," Mrs. Belden said. "Please take Bobby with you. He'll help you keep your mind off other things."

"Oh, Moms!" Trixie tried to explain. "It's just that—"

"I know," Mrs. Belden said patiently. "I don't want anything else to happen to Ethel Elliot, either. But there's nothing to suggest that anything else *will* happen. If we act as if we expect something, we'll only cause the poor dear needless worry."

After finishing their chores, Trixie, Brian, and Mart headed for the lake on the Wheeler estate. They wore their swimsuits under their clothes, since someone often got pushed into the water before he or she had a chance to change. At the boathouse, Mart made a lunge for Trixie, but she dodged out of the way and *he* splashed into the lake. Laughing and shouting, the others got out of jeans and shirts before joining him in the water.

The *Water Witch,* Jim's large rowboat, was their diving platform and resting place—for as long as anyone could keep from being thrown overboard.

When Di arrived, there was a contest to see who could stay underwater the longest. Jim lasted for two minutes. Surprisingly, Di almost matched that time. Brian was a close third, and Mart was next. Trixie and Honey tied for last place.

"The girls should have won," Brian said as everyone except Trixie and Honey relaxed in the rowboat. "It's a scientifically proven medical fact that women require less oxygen than men, so—"

Mart hooted. "Never mind the facts! It's a simple matter of predilection to loquaciousness. Trix and Honey just couldn't stand to keep quiet long enough!"

Trixie reached up over the gunwale and

grabbed Mart's leg. Honey reached for his other leg.

"Give him a push, Di!" Trixie screamed.

The rowboat rocked wildly. With too many struggling people on one side, the gunwale dipped under, and water poured in. The boat capsized, spilling everyone in a laughing, splashing tangle.

Rolling the boat over upright, the Bob-Whites reached in with cupped hands and began bailing. Much of the water went back into the boat as they slapped it at one another.

"This'll go faster if I can work with both hands," Mart panted. He started to hoist himself into the boat. The gunwale went under again and the boat filled up once more.

"Big help you are!" Trixie declared.

"Let's take it into the shallows," Jim suggested. "Everybody grab hold with one hand and swim. Somebody get the oars."

Brian and Honey each got an oar and stowed them in the swamped boat. Kicking and stroking with free arms, they gradually moved the waterlogged boat toward shore.

When the water was only hip-deep, they stood up and began bailing again with cupped hands. They were too exhausted and breathless for any more horseplay.

Trixie felt her feet sinking into the soft bed of the lake. Something beneath her right foot gave way slightly, and a rush of bubbles brushed her ankles. Trixie shuddered.

"What's the matter?" Jim asked.

"Nothing," said Trixie. "It's just squishy on the bottom."

Standing together on one side of the boat, the young people tipped it on its side to dump out most of the remaining water.

"Be careful getting aboard," Jim advised. "I'm too pooped to go through that again!"

"Wait." Brian waded toward something in the water. It was a brown envelope. "Who does this belong to? Was it in the boat?"

"I didn't bring it," said Trixie.

"It's not mine," said Honey.

Di shook her head.

Brian turned the envelope over to see if it was addressed. "We'll soon find out—" He gaped in amazement at the envelope. "I can't believe this."

"What?" Trixie asked. "Who's it addressed to?"

"Charles Hartman," Brian said slowly, still staring at the envelope.

"He lives up on Glen Road," said Trixie in disbelief. "What would an envelope addressed to him be doing in the Wheelers' lake?"

"Here, you take a look for yourself," Brian said. He extended the soggy brown envelope to Trixie.

The envelope was imprinted in black with the words DELIVER BY THIRD DAY OF MONTH. Charles Hartman's name and address showed through the little window in front. There was no stamp; the envelope had a postage-paid impression. When Trixie's eyes shifted to the return address in the upper left corner, she yelped.

"This is from Social Security!" she exclaimed. "It's Mr. Hartman's Social Security check!"

Di screamed with excitement, pointing. "There's another one!"

Jim plunged into the water and held up another brown envelope. "This one still has the check in it, too!"

"Where are they coming from?" Honey asked.

"The bottom of the lake," Trixie cried. "I stepped on something when we were bailing out the boat. Where were we then?"

"Out there," Brian said. "About where Jim is."

Jim, hip-deep in water, squatted and put his face below the surface. Trixie pushed forward, sweeping herself under. She opened her eyes and peered through murky water stirred up by all the activity. Tiny fish glinted like diamonds in the sunlight filtering into the water. Trixie pulled herself deeper, searching the bottom. Honey, her hair streaming, appeared beside her. Trixie surfaced to gulp air.

"We're too far out," she called.

Before she could plunge under again, Jim shouted. "Wait! Let's get organized. Mart, over here, to the right of Trixie. Di, Honey"—he pointed—"form a line, about an arm's length

65

apart. Everybody ready? All right, let's work our way in."

The line of B.W.G.'s dipped below the surface, and the young people swam toward the shore, scanning the lake bottom.

Now we're getting too far in, Trixie thought. Then she spotted something. Her legs propelled her outstretched hand closer. It was a torn paper bag, and it was filled with brown envelopes. Sliding both hands under it, Trixie felt a large stone that had been used to weight the bag and make it sink. She planted her feet in the slimy bottom and stood up, gently lifting her discovery clear of the water.

"I found it!" she cried.

Wading shoreward, Trixie stepped on a rock and tottered. Jim grasped her arm to support her. At the water's edge, Trixie placed the sodden, torn bag on the grassy bank.

"Those must be the stolen Social Security checks!" Brian declared.

Trixie nodded. "I don't remember how many names I read in the paper, but I'll bet all of their checks are right here."

Jim was spreading the envelopes on the grass. "They're all Glen Road addresses," he said.

"How did they get in the lake?" Di asked in a puzzled tone.

"I'll bet they were thrown in," Trixie said. "With this stone to make the bag sink. When I stepped on the bag and broke it, one of the envelopes floated to the surface."

"But why would anyone want to throw them in the lake?" Di wondered. "It couldn't have been to hide them."

Brian shook his head. "It doesn't make sense. Why would anyone steal checks and then throw them away?"

"Incriminating evidence," Mart suggested. "Maybe the thief thought he was going to be caught, so he disposed of the checks."

"That makes sense," Trixie said. Maybe Mrs. Elliot *had* seen the thief and scared him. The arson attempt was to keep her quiet. Then Trixie remembered what her mother had said: Mrs. Elliot wouldn't keep quiet about anything illegal. "On the other hand, maybe it doesn't make sense," Trixie said slowly.

Jim gathered the envelopes. "We'd better no-
tify Sergeant Molinson. Maybe he can come up
with an answer."

"If Trixie hasn't already got it," Mart said.

"Not yet," Trixie admitted. "Not yet. . . ."

Mr. Hartman's Secret • 4

WHEN SERGEANT MOLINSON ARRIVED, he
frowned at the envelopes drying out in the sun
on the boathouse dock.

"You shouldn't have moved them from where
you found them," he grumbled. "Too late now.
Show me where, and let's hope you didn't destroy any other evidence that might have been
in the area."

Trixie smiled impishly. "Jim, you're closest
to the sergeant's size. Have you got an extra

pair of swimming trunks to lend him?"

Molinson scowled at her.

Trixie broadened her smile. "We found them at the bottom of the lake. They were in a bag, weighted with that stone."

"Oh!" Molinson grunted.

Jim grinned. "You can change in the boat-house, Sergeant. I'll dig out a pair of trunks."

"That won't be necessary," Molinson said.

Trixie thought that this would be a good opportunity for her to confirm her suspicions, while Molinson was off guard. "Someone along Glen Road must have seen the checks being stolen," she said. "That's probably why they were tossed in the lake, to get rid of incriminating evidence. When we find out who—"

"Nobody saw anything," Molinson said curtly, cutting her off. "My officers questioned everyone along Glen Road after the checks were reported stolen. And what do you mean by 'we,' young lady?"

Trixie gulped. "There must be some reason why the checks were thrown away instead of being cashed," she said.

"Of course," Molinson said noncommittally.

Trixie waited, but he didn't continue. He carefully gathered the envelopes. "Suppose you show me exactly where you found these."

"Out there, sir." Jim pointed toward the opposite side of the lake. "I'll row you out."

Molinson eyed the rowboat and shook his head. "I'll drive around. One of you come with me." He nodded at Jim.

"Better take Trixie," Jim suggested. "She was the one who found them. She can show you where they were, and maybe you can get some idea about where they were thrown in."

Molinson hesitated.

Brian spoke up. "I'll drive Trixie around in the club car."

"Okay," Molinson said.

As they walked up to the garage, Trixie muttered to Brian, "What's the big idea? I wanted to see if he'd tell me any more about how his investigation's coming."

"I know," Brian admitted.

"Then why?"

Brian stopped and faced Trixie. "Because

there's a police rule against a male officer transporting a woman in a police car without having a policewoman as an escort."

Trixie protested. "But that doesn't apply to—"

Brian smiled at her. "You're not a little girl anymore, sis. You're a young woman."

Trixie stared at him. He wasn't kidding.

"Gee, thanks . . . I think."

A few minutes later, Brian parked the B.W.G. station wagon behind the police car at the edge of Glen Road.

"Let's not rile the sergeant by tramping all over his evidence," he advised. "Let's wait until he asks us to get out."

Rain and traffic in the past ten days had destroyed any possible indication that a car might have stopped along the road near the lake. Sergeant Molinson scanned the area carefully, then began walking slowly toward the lake. He beckoned for Brian and Trixie to follow.

At the water's edge, Trixie pointed to the spot where she had found the bag of checks. Molinson mumbled that the bag had probably been tossed there with an underhand throw.

A search of the shore revealed nothing.

Molinson gave Trixie a wry look. "It's not like television, where there are clues all around, just waiting to be noticed. Real detective work isn't so quick and easy."

Trixie raised her eyebrows. "But it's exciting anyway," she declared.

Molinson snorted. "You call *this* exciting? Listen: Stick to television, kid."

That stung. Trixie didn't feel as grown-up as she had a few minutes before.

"Whoever threw those checks in certainly didn't expect them to be found," Molinson went on. "And I do owe you my thanks for that. But I don't think finding the checks will solve anything."

Back in the station wagon, Trixie motioned for Brian not to start the engine. "Let Sergeant Molinson leave first," she said.

"What's up?" Brian asked, puzzled. They watched as the police car headed back to Sleepyside.

Trixie opened the glove compartment and

73

removed a pad and pencil. "Help me remember as many names as we can from those checks," she said.

"The names were all in last week's paper," Brian reminded her. "We can go back to Honey's and dig it out and—"

"And Miss Trask will want to know what we're up to," Trixie interrupted. "She won't let Honey come back with us anyway, and since we're already here. . . ."

"What now?" Brian prompted.

Trixie was jotting names on the pad. "If we could find out where the last check was stolen," she said thoughtfully, "maybe we could discover who or what scared the thief into getting rid of the evidence."

"But Sergeant Molinson said—"

"I know what he said," Trixie stated. "But there must be *some* reason why the thief threw the checks away. Drive down Glen Road, slowly, while I check the names on the mailboxes."

"Okay," Brian said. "The others won't be expecting us back right away. I hope."

As Brian drove along Glen Road, Trixie

called out the names on the mailboxes. Frequently the name didn't sound familiar, but that could be because there was no reason for it to be recalled. Not every mailbox received a Social Security check each month. Still, there were a number of older people living in the area.

Another mailbox came into view. "Charles Hartman," Trixie said, checking it off the list. "His was the first envelope we found floating in the lake."

The next mailbox, around a turn in the road, was Mrs. Elliot's. Brian drove on by it. In about a quarter of a mile, they passed another box. The name wasn't on Trixie's list, and neither of them remembered it from the checks. Two more mailboxes, side by side, came into view. Trixie read the names aloud.

"I know the last one doesn't belong on the list," Brian said. "Their son is a classmate of mine. No old folks living in his home."

"It's not just older people who get Social Security checks," Trixie said. "Disabled people and widows—"

"Both parents are alive and healthy," Brian said. He squinted at the other box. "I think there's an older couple living across the road." He pointed toward a little house set back among the trees. "I'll see if I can find out anything."

Brian parked the station wagon beside the road and got out. Trixie could see him talking first to an elderly woman at the door, then to an old man who joined them.

When Brian returned to the car, he looked thoughtful. "Their check wasn't stolen, but it could have been. It sat in the box for hours before one of them came down to get the mail. And they told me they've got friends up the road a bit, and none of them had their checks stolen!"

Trixie stared at him. "That can only mean one thing," she declared. "The thief didn't get beyond Charles Hartman's box."

"Or," Brian suggested, "maybe he did get as far as Mrs. Elliot's. Maybe you *are* right—she saw him and scared him off. That might explain yesterday's arson attempt!"

"Let's go back to Mrs. Elliot's," Trixie urged.

76

Brian was already turning the station wagon around. At Mrs. Elliot's cottage, Max Elliot came to the door in response to Trixie's knock.

"She isn't here," he said, when Trixie asked for Mrs. Elliot. "She drove into town."

Trixie hesitated. "Maybe you can tell me what I wanted to know."

Max waited. Trixie took a deep breath and continued. "Did anything . . . uh, unusual happen ten days ago? June third? It might have been in the early afternoon, right after the mail was delivered. Did Mrs. Elliot—"

"She wasn't here," Max interrupted. "She was down in White Plains, delivering an order of flowers."

"Oh." Trixie paused. Max eyed her curiously. "Max, did *you* go down to the box to get the mail that day? Maybe you saw—"

Max shook his head. "I wasn't here either. I drove her to White Plains."

"Oh," Trixie repeated.

Max looked puzzled. "What are you trying to find out?"

Trixie sighed. "The Social Security checks

were stolen on Glen Road only as far as Charles Hartman's box, the one before yours. We thought that maybe Mrs. Elliot, or you, had seen the thief and scared him into getting rid of the evidence. We found the checks today."

Max blinked at her. "You found the checks?"

Trixie nodded.

Max pursed his lips. "Guess you're on the right track, then. Someone must have scared him into getting rid of them. But it couldn't have been here. Maybe someone hasn't told the police what they saw."

"Maybe," Trixie murmured.

Max eyed her. "Why are you interested in the stolen checks?"

Trixie wasn't so sure anymore. She didn't want to mention her suspicion about the arson attempt. "Honey Wheeler and I are going to have our own detective agency someday," she said. "Well, thanks for your help."

Max shrugged. "What help?"

"You pointed me in a new direction," Trixie said. "Thanks again."

Brian looked at her, curious, as they went

back to the station wagon.

"Let's go see Charles Hartman," Trixie said.

"Are you sure you want to?" Brian asked. "If Sergeant Molinson finds out that you've been—"

"I just want to meet Mr. Hartman," Trixie said unconvincingly. "After all, his was the first check we found."

Brian shook his head. "Okay. But be careful what you say."

Minutes later, Trixie and Brian were standing on the Hartmans' porch. A cheerful-looking white-haired lady, leaning on a cane, answered the door. The Beldens introduced themselves.

"How nice to have someone calling," Mrs. Hartman said. "Do come in."

"I hope we're not disturbing you," Trixie said.

"Not at all, not at all. I was just watching television. I can't do much of anything else these days. One of those soap operas, where they suffer and suffer—makes me thankful for how blessed I am." She made her way across the neat living room to turn off the TV.

"Oh, don't," Trixie protested. "You'll miss some of the story."

"It'll be easy to pick up tomorrow or the next day." Mrs. Hartman chuckled. "It'll drag out for weeks. They never solve their problems quickly."

A step sounded on the porch. Mrs. Hartman turned toward the door. "Charley, come in. We've got visitors. Wipe your feet first."

"Do I dare forget?" Charles Hartman came into the room with a smile. Unlike his wife, he stood erect and was lean and catlike. Only his white hair betrayed his age.

"I was out back chopping wood," he said. "Heard you drive up, so I thought I'd be nosy." He winked. "I have to check up on who might be calling on my beautiful bride."

"Charley!" Mrs. Hartman blushed. She spoke happily to Trixie and Brian. "Nearly fifty years we've been married. He still acts like it was yesterday."

"That's beautiful," Trixie said.

"She's beautiful," Hartman corrected, looking at his wife.

Trixie felt guilty. The Hartmans were a cheerful, charming couple. They weren't the type to withhold information from the police. Still, though, Mr. Hartman's check had been the last one stolen. . . .

"Well," Trixie began as they all sat down, "we're sort of friends of Mrs. Elliot's. We—our family, I mean—have known Mrs. Elliot for a long time. We were there visiting yesterday. Since her husband died, Mrs. Elliot has been having a hard time with her flower business, so it's a good thing that her Social Security check—"

Trixie stopped. Charles Hartman was regarding her with steady, probing steel blue eyes. She floundered and forgot what she was trying to say.

"Young lady," Charles Hartman said bluntly, "quit circling around like a buzzard and get to the point."

"Charley!" his wife admonished.

"Be quiet, sweetheart," he said, still looking at Trixie. "This isn't just a casual social visit. This young lady is after something. Well?" he asked Trixie.

Trixie wished she could dig a hole and get

81

into it. "We—I mean, I was wondering . . . on the day that the Social Security checks were stolen . . . if you told Sergeant Molinson—"

"I told him I couldn't offer any help. What do you think I should have said?" He waited a moment for Trixie to answer. "Well?"

Trixie reddened. "I thought maybe Mrs. Elliot saw something, but she—"

"You're circling again. Get to the point."

Trixie took a deep breath. "We made a list of people who had their checks stolen. It looks like yours was the last one taken, because the other checks delivered on Glen Road past here were received. We found the stolen checks today in the Wheelers' lake."

Hartman nodded. "Go on. Why did you come here?"

"The thief must have been scared away from what he was doing," Trixie said. "Somebody must have seen him. Why else would he try to get rid of the checks?"

Hartman smiled grimly. "So," he said, "since my check was apparently the last one stolen, you thought that I might have seen the thief."

Trixie nodded.

"And," Hartman went on, "that if I had seen him, I deliberately avoided saying so to the police."

Trixie nodded again. "I'm sorry, sir."

"None of that," Hartman said brusquely. "When you're following a lead, you've got to follow it with no apologies."

Trixie stared at him.

He laughed. "I'm an ex-cop. I'd still be on the Albany police force if they didn't have mandatory retirement rules." He turned to Brian. "Come here a minute, young man. I want to show you something."

Puzzled, Brian got out of his chair and walked toward Hartman. Suddenly, in a blur of motion, Hartman was out of his own chair and holding Brian in an armlock from behind. "Squirm out of it, boy," Hartman urged. "Remember, I'm an old man."

Brian tried to free himself, first halfheartedly, then in earnest. He could not get loose.

Hartman released him and patted Brian's back. "I'm also an ex-judo instructor," he said with a grin. "If I'd seen the thief, I'd have turned him over to Molinson . . . with a broken arm."

Brian nodded vigorously, gingerly rubbing his shoulder.

"I'm usually waiting at the mailbox for the mailman when the checks are delivered," Hartman said. "But that day, I was getting too many laughs watching something on TV with my bride." He regarded Trixie. "Why are you so interested in checks stolen from old people?"

Trixie explained how she and Honey hoped to be detectives someday. She also told about the arson attempt. "We thought that it was a warning, because Mrs. Elliot had seen the thief."

Hartman nodded.

"But Mrs. Elliot couldn't have seen him," Trixie went on. "She was in White Plains that day. So was Max."

"And," Brian added, "nobody farther up Glen Road saw him. No checks were stolen there."

Trixie scratched her head. "Now it looks like there's no connection at all between the stolen checks and the arson attempt. But why else would anybody do such a terrible thing to Mrs. Elliot?"

Hartman was deep in thought. "If Sam Elliot were still alive, then I'd think—" He stopped as Trixie leaned forward to hear what he was going to say.

"No," Hartman said. "Ethel Elliot is a good neighbor and a good friend. Her husband's dead, so there's no sense in bringing his name into this. You forget that I even mentioned it. Understand?"

"But—" Trixie began.

"Forget it," Hartman said. It was final.

Dan's Discovery • 5

JUNE LED THE WAY into July. But the clues that
Trixie and Honey had hoped to pursue led no-
where. There was no answer to the question of
why the checks had been stolen and then
thrown away. There was no solution to the
arson attempt. Mr. Hartman's comment about
Sam Elliot nagged at Trixie's mind, but there
was no answer for that, either.

To make things more frustrating, Trixie was
grounded—not as punishment, but because Jim

and Brian were away as counselors at a boys' camp. That left the Bob-Whites without a driver, since Dan, who had just got his driver's license, was usually too busy helping Mr. Maypenny.

Trixie was doing "overtime" baby-sitting because her mother was organizing the garden club to participate in a flower contest sponsored by a White Plains newspaper.

Trixie asked about it one day as they prepared lunch. "What's the contest all about, Moms?"

"It's a photography contest," Mrs. Belden said. "The photographs must have something to do with flowers and horticulture."

"In case you don't know," Mart said grandly, *"horticulture* means—"

"I know what it means," Trixie said. "It's what you want to get into. Right, earthworm?"

"Worm!" Bobby repeated.

"Bobby," Mrs. Belden chided. "Don't call your brother names."

"Trixie just did! But I wasn't calling him a worm. Trixie made me think we ought to dig some worms and go fishing this afternoon."

"Later, Bobby," Trixie sighed. "You said pictures of flowers, Moms?"

"There'll be various categories, from views of whole gardens to just a single flower. The contest will run for several weeks, and each week, the best entry will be published in the paper. Those become eligible for the big prizes to be awarded at the end of the contest."

"Is it only for amateur gardeners?" Trixie asked.

"No, because it's really a photography contest with the theme of flowers. It *is* restricted to amateur photographers."

"Then," Trixie suggested, "Mrs. Elliot could enter if she wanted to."

"Of course. And I hope she does. A photograph of her sweet peas climbing on an umbrella frame would certainly be interesting."

"Hey!" Mart exclaimed. "Here's a title for her entry: Sweet Idea for Sweet Peas."

Trixie looked at him. "Sometimes you do say something that makes sense."

"That was pretty good," Mart declared.

Trixie turned back to her mother. "I'll bet they'd have won the contest for sure if Sam Elliot were still alive. He was quite a horticulturist, wasn't he?" she said, giving Mart a look as she used the word.

"He certainly was," Mrs. Belden agreed. "He raised several unusual plants and flowers. There was a truck from the city almost every day, picking up orders." Mrs. Belden frowned. "That's why it's so difficult to understand why there wasn't much left for Ethel after he died. Just the property."

Peter Belden came in. "Sorry I'm late for lunch," he apologized. "Got held up at the bank."

"You were held up?" Bobby asked excitedly.

"Not that way, thank goodness." His father turned to Mrs. Belden as Bobby, having lost interest in the conversation, left the room. "I heard you mentioning Ethel Elliot. As a matter of fact, she's why I'm late," Mr. Belden went on.

"Did she come to see you?" Trixie asked anxiously.

"Trixie," Mrs. Belden said, "that's none of our

business." But she looked inquiringly at Peter.

He sighed, shaking his head. "Bank business is private, of course. But I know you're all concerned about Ethel Elliot." He paused, looking at each of them. "What I say is to stay at this table and go no farther. Ethel Elliot came to me for a loan. She needs a new pump for her well. She wanted something short-term that she could pay off quickly."

"What happened to her old pump?" Trixie asked.

Peter Belden shrugged his shoulders. "It ran dry. It wasn't pulling water anymore. That can ruin a pump."

"Poor Ethel," Mrs. Belden said. "She's just barely getting by as it is. Did you grant her the loan?"

"Not the way she wanted it," Peter Belden said. "I had to extend it to make the payments smaller, or she wouldn't have had any money to live on. A one-and-a-half horsepower self-priming pump costs more than three hundred dollars."

"And on top of that, she's going to have to

pay the interest on the loan," said Mrs. Belden.

Trixie's father nodded. "It's going to be hard, I know. I did the best I could for her. I offered to lend her the money myself, but she wouldn't hear of it."

"You did what you could, Daddy," said Trixie. "Now Mrs. Elliot really needs to enter that contest—and win!"

Mrs. Belden frowned. "Trixie, don't build up false hopes. I'm sure Ethel doesn't even own a camera."

Trixie took a bite of her sandwich and chewed thoughtfully. "Daddy," she asked after a moment, "can Mart borrow your camera?"

"Hey! Stop putting words in my mouth," Mart objected.

"Mart," Trixie pleaded, "you're so much better with a camera than I am."

Mart gaped at her. "Did I hear words of adulation?"

"And," Trixie continued, "as a future earthwor—as a future horticulturist, you'll know how to photograph flowers to best advantage. *Prize-winning* advantage."

91

"Give up, Mart." Peter Belden chuckled. "You haven't got a chance. I know from experience." He glanced from Trixie to her mother.

"What does that mean, Peter?" Mrs. Belden asked with mock severity.

"It means I've got a wonderful family, always ready to do something good for others." He turned to Mart. "You know I'm fussy about my camera. Take good care of it."

Mart nodded.

"Daddy," Trixie said, "it's strange that Mr. Elliot didn't leave his wife much money when he died. Didn't he have anything in the bank?"

"That's private, Trixie. But Sam Elliot didn't bank here in Sleepyside anyway. As far as I know, he didn't bank anywhere. Since he didn't leave a will, several banks were contacted to see if he had accounts. None were found."

"Maybe he hid his money somewhere," Mart suggested.

Peter Belden pointed a finger at Mart. "Now, don't go—"

"—jumping to conclusions," Trixie finished for her father, trying to hide the excitement she suddenly felt. "May I be excused?" she asked, pushing back her chair. "I want to call Honey. If Dan's there, maybe he'll drive us to Mrs. Elliot's this afternoon so Mart can take a picture of the sweet peas." She hurried from the room.

"Yes," Honey said over the phone a minute later, "Dan is here. He's having lunch with Regan. What are you so excited about, Trixie?"

"I'll tell you in a minute," Trixie said. "Ask Dan if he'll *please* drive us to Mrs. Elliot's this afternoon."

"Okay. Hang on."

It seemed like an hour while Trixie waited for Honey to return to the phone.

"Trixie? Dan said he'd drive us. Come on over after lunch. Now, what's up?"

"We're in business again," Trixie said excitedly. "Wear some grubbies—we may do some digging."

"You mean asking more questions?" Honey queried.

"No, I mean *digging*," Trixie said. "See you in a while."

When Trixie hung up the phone and turned around, Mart was standing right beside her.

"If you think you fooled Dad and Moms, you're wrong," he said.

Trixie was dismayed. "Did they say we couldn't go to Mrs. Elliot's?"

"They think the idea of helping her enter the contest is a noble one," Mart said. "But they don't find solace in the sound of the wild-goose wings flapping in your head. Or the glint of buried treasure in your eyes."

"Oh, stop," Trixie insisted. "Can we go or not?"

"Yes. With conditions."

"What conditions?" Trixie asked.

"I'm to clip the wings of the wild geese if necessary," Mart said.

"You're always trying to do that anyway," Trixie retorted.

"Albeit in a brotherly way." Mart grinned. "This time I have a parental mandate behind me."

"Just keep it back there, out of my way," Trixie warned.

"There's more," Mart said.

Trixie eyed him suspiciously. "Such as?"

"Bobby is to go with us."

Trixie accepted the news calmly, knowing she had no choice. "Okay. He's probably tired of being read to and playing games." She brightened. "Besides, he can keep Mrs. Elliot company while we—"

"Clip-clip! Clip-clip!" Mart made scissors motions with two fingers.

As they walked up the hill to the Wheelers', Bobby scampered ahead and tried to turn up-hill somersaults.

"Easy," Trixie cautioned. "If you get too dirty or hurt yourself, you'll have to go home." She spoke to Mart, who carried his father's Leica camera on its strap around his neck. "This picture will be important, so make it good. It just has to win a prize. Try for sharp detail and good balance."

Mart scowled at her. "Elementary, my dear sister. But why the exhortation? You've already admitted that I have quite an overwhelming superiority with photographic apparatus."

Dan and Honey were waiting on the lawn near the B.W.G. station wagon. Bobby dashed toward them and crashed into Dan, who then tumbled backward on the grass.

"Wow!" Dan shouted. "Did you see that tackle by the junior linebacker?"

Bobby yelled with delight and charged again. Dan took a stance, only to be tumbled over once more.

On the way to Mrs. Elliot's, Dan told Bobby about twin fawns he had seen on the Wheeler game preserve. Bobby told Dan about a dragon he had seen behind the Beldens' shed.

Dan laughed. "What an imagination!"

"It runs in the family," Mart commented dryly. "With some members," he added, glancing at Trixie, "it's really running wild today. So watch out."

"Oh?" Dan inquired with a smile. "I thought this was just a photographic expedition."

"It is," Mart said. "But it's also a reconnaissance mission. Now Trixie thinks there's buried treasure at the Elliot place."

"I didn't say that!" Trixie declared. "*You* were the one who said that at lunch."

"I just happened to say the words before you could," Mart said. "As I recall, your mouth was full at the time."

"Treasure!" Honey said excitedly. "Is that what you meant about doing some digging?"

Trixie told Honey and Dan about the conversation at lunch—omitting the part about Mrs. Elliot's loan. "Moms said that Mr. Elliot was doing well with his business. But when he died, there was hardly anything left for Mrs. Elliot. And Dad said that Mr. Elliot didn't put any money in the bank. That's when Mart said that maybe the money was hidden at the Elliots'."

"I was just babbling," Mart said. "Listen, Trixie: Mrs. Elliot digs up that whole place every spring. If there was money buried there, don't you think she would have found it by now?"

"Mart has a point there, Trixie," Honey said.

"Maybe it's hidden in one of the buildings," Trixie persisted.

"Mrs. Elliot probably uses the shed every day

97

during the summer," Honey pointed out. "So if it was hidden there, she would have found it, too."

Mart snorted. "If it is hidden in the shed, then whoever tried to set that fire sure didn't know about it!"

"Of course not," Trixie stated. "If he knew about the hidden money, then why would he steal the Social Security checks?"

"Hey! Slow down a minute," Dan said. "You lost me back there. Trixie, are you saying that the man who tried to set the fire is the same man who stole the checks?"

"Yes," Trixie said.

"Do you have any proof of that?" Dan asked in a serious tone.

"Well . . . no," Trixie admitted. "Just that the check thief and the arsonist both ended up at the same place: Mrs. Elliot's."

"That doesn't mean a thing," Dan snapped. He was no longer as easygoing as he had been minutes before. "Besides, from what you told us, the check thief only went as far as the Hartmans'."

Honey made a sign for Trixie to keep quiet. "Dan's right," she said in a soothing tone. "There's probably no connection at all."

Trixie, Honey, and Mart exchanged glances. Mart shrugged his shoulders.

When Dan swung the station wagon onto Mrs. Elliot's drive, he seemed relieved that they had arrived. As they were piling out, Mrs. Elliot appeared on the porch.

"Well, hello," she said. "What a nice surprise. Bobby! I've hardly seen you since you were a baby."

"I'm all growed up now," Bobby said with pride.

"So you are, so you are." Mrs. Elliot came down the steps. "I was expecting Max, and when I heard your car, I thought he'd come back." Her gaze sought Honey. "Does your mother need to buy some more flowers?"

Honey shook her head. "Mother's out of town again with my father."

"Oh," Mrs. Elliot said, attempting to hide her disappointment.

"We did come about flowers, though," Trixie

said quickly. "Have you heard about the flower photography contest sponsored by the White Plains paper? There are going to be prizes. We think you should enter; you've got such beautiful flowers."

"Thank you, Trixie." Mrs. Elliot smiled wanly. "But I don't own a camera. Even if I did have one, I wouldn't know how to use it."

"Moms said she was pretty sure you didn't have one. We brought my father's camera. Mart's a real expert with it—"

Mart interrupted. "Remember, you said that in front of witnesses."

"And," Trixie went on, "we'd like to take some pictures and enter them for you."

"Well, bless you," Mrs. Elliot said. "Go right ahead. But the pictures should be entered in your names, since you're taking them."

"But they're your flowers," Trixie said. "We think a picture of the way you grow your sweet peas would surely win."

"Take all the pictures you wish. And be sure to pick yourself a bouquet of sweet peas, too. Since I don't know anything about taking pictures, I'll stay out of your way. Want to help me prepare some lemonade and a plate of cookies, Bobby?"

Bobby nodded. "Daddy won't let me touch his camera, either."

"If there's anything you need, let me know," Mrs. Elliot told Mart. "I'll tell Dan where to get it if Max hasn't come back with the new water pump."

"What happened to the pump you had?" Trixie asked, pretending not to know.

"It wasn't drawing water. Neither Max nor I noticed until too late. Without water running through it, a pump gets hot." Mrs. Elliot shook her head. "It froze up and caused the electric motor to burn itself out. I had to buy a whole new pump."

Mrs. Elliot turned and led Bobby into the cottage.

Trixie sighed. "She's got to have a pump to water all the flowers. She'd be out of business without it. What would make a pump go bad so suddenly?"

"Stop spreading those wild-goose wings,"

Mart cautioned. "Who said it went bad suddenly? Maybe she knew it needed repairs but just didn't have the money for it. Maybe she just kept hoping it would hold out, like some people do with cars and washing machines and—"

"All right," Trixie said impatiently. "Leave *some* feathers on my wings. Put your mind, such as it is, to taking some good pictures."

The sweet pea vines were a lovely mass of variegated color, climbing up and over the suspended umbrella frame.

"Oh, look at them!" Trixie exclaimed softly. "They're even more beautiful than the last time I saw them. Be sure to get the umbrella frame in the picture, Mart."

Trixie's eyes drank in the colors: white, blue, pink, yellow, lavender, and red. Suddenly she looked worried. "Mart, the camera is loaded with *color* film, isn't it?"

Mart gaped at her. "I thought you wanted black-and-white."

"I did not!" Trixie screamed. Then she detected the beginning of his grin. "Ooooooh, you—you—"

"I'm the camera expert, remember? You said it yourself," Mart reminded her.

"You should have taken a picture of the expression on Trixie's face," Honey said with a giggle.

"The aperture would have atrophied," Mart declared.

"I'll aprofy your atrochure!" Trixie warned.

"Stand back, please," Mart cautioned. "Expert at work." He peered through the viewfinder.

"The vines hide the umbrella frame too much," he said. "Dan, will you find a ladder or something and get up there and clear the frame a bit?"

Dan looked in the shed and found a ladder. Trixie steadied it for him as he climbed to clear some of the flowers and vines from the umbrella frame.

"That's good," Mart said.

As Mart began photographing, Dan nodded toward the shed. "As long as we're here, I can help Max install the new pump if he gets back in time," he said. "I'm going to go take a look at the old pump."

Trixie nodded, watching intently as Mart changed camera angles.

A few minutes later, when Trixie glanced up, she saw Dan at the B.W.G. station wagon. He looked in the glove compartment, then moved to the rear and opened the tailgate. He opened the storage compartment and rummaged around.

Trixie couldn't see what was in his hand as he moved away from the wagon and disappeared behind the shed.

"Dan's up to something," she whispered to Honey, not wanting Mart to overhear. "I'm going to go see what. When Mart's done taking pictures, you cut the bouquet Mrs. Elliot said we could have."

"I'll go with you," Honey murmured.

"No," Trixie said softly. "Mart will suspect we're up to something then."

"All right," Honey agreed reluctantly. "But let me know what's happening."

"Of course, partner." Then Trixie raised her voice. "It's hot out here. I'll go see if Mrs. Elliot and Bobby have the lemonade ready."

"Good idea," Mart declared, lining up another shot.

Trixie started toward the house, then cut through the garden toward the shed. She found Dan kneeling beside the faded red housing of an electric water pump on a cement slab. He was frowning.

"What's the matter, Dan?" Trixie asked.

Dan started, then motioned her down beside him. "Don't let Mart squelch your imagination anymore," he said. "This pump didn't wear itself out. It was sabotaged!"

A Series of "Accidents" • 6

SABOTAGED?" Trixie stared at Dan. "How can you tell?"

She looked at the pump. It was housed in a faded red metal box with two pipe attachments, one for drawing water and the other for pumping it out. At one side of the box, a cylinder with an on/off switch enclosed the electric motor. Except for its obvious age, Trixie could see nothing wrong with the pump or motor.

"When Mart asked me to find a ladder," Dan

said, "I saw the pump here. I thought I could help Max install the new one, just like I said. I came back to see if this one was disconnected, and, well . . . I started wondering."

"About what?" Trixie asked.

Dan pointed to the pump. "These things are really pretty simple inside. Just a few moving parts. While it's pumping, the water that it draws helps to keep it cool. Since it hadn't been drawing water, I wondered if maybe the well had been pumped dry. We haven't had much rain, so I thought maybe the underground water table had dropped. I rummaged around in the station wagon until I found some fishline and a sinker."

"So that's what I saw you doing," Trixie said.

"You don't miss much, do you," Dan acknowledged. He nodded toward the well. It wasn't the picturesque type with a shingled roof and a wooden bucket on a rope. It was simply a cement slab surrounding a steel pipe six inches in diameter.

"I lowered the line and sinker into it," Dan explained. "This pump should be able to draw

107

water up from about forty feet. So when I had about fifty feet of line down the well, I began pulling it up, about three feet at a time, feeling for the first sign of wetness."

Trixie nodded, understanding. "How far down was the water level?"

"Nine feet. I only pulled the line up three times before it was wet."

"Only nine feet!" Trixie exclaimed.

"Obviously there's plenty of water," Dan said. "So then I figured that there wasn't any water in the suction line."

He pointed to a pipe about two inches in diameter that descended into the well. The pipe took a right-angled bend a few inches above the ground and then extended horizontally over toward the pump.

"If there's nothing wrong with the suction line," Dan continued, "there should be water in it all the way up to the pump, higher than the water level of the well. There's a valve at the bottom of the pipe that keeps the water from dropping back into the well when the pump isn't running."

Trixie nodded again and pointed to the elbow where the pipe made a bend toward the pump. "If there's nothing wrong with the valve at the bottom, the water should be up to here now. Right?"

"Right," Dan said. "And it is."

"But the pump still wasn't drawing water," Trixie said in a confused tone. "I don't understand."

"I didn't, either," Dan admitted. "But there had to be some reason why the pump suddenly stopped drawing water and ruined itself."

Dan placed his hand on the underside of the pipe where it extended horizontally from the well to the pump. "Feel the pipe."

Trixie touched the cold smoothness of the pipe. As she slid her hand along underneath it, the tips of her fingers went into a notched opening.

"That opening let air in," Dan explained. "The pump was pulling air instead of water, and that's what wrecked it."

"That's not a crack," Trixie said. "It's too smooth."

"It was done with a metal file," Dan confirmed. "I stuck my head under to have a look. Somebody filed a hole in that pipe. It was deliberately sabotaged."

Trixie scowled. "First the arson attempt, and now this. Someone is definitely trying to ruin Mrs. Elliot's flower business. But who? And why?"

"What about Max?" Dan asked.

Trixie shook her head. "He was working in the cornfield during the arson attempt," she reminded him.

"That doesn't mean he couldn't have known about it," Dan pointed out.

"But he was so mad—" Trixie began.

"Maybe he was mad at *you* for preventing the fire," Dan said.

Trixie pondered that for a moment. "Why would Max do those things to his own stepmother?" she asked.

Dan shrugged. "It doesn't make any sense, does it?" He stood up and brushed off his knees. Trixie stood, too.

"There's something I'd better tell you," Dan

said slowly. "It's been bothering me for a long time now."

Trixie nodded. "I knew *something* was wrong, Dan."

Dan grinned slightly. "Was it that obvious? I'm sorry. It's just that I didn't want you and Honey getting involved in something that could be really dangerous."

Trixie raised her eyebrows, curious.

"I was in town on the day of the arson attempt," Dan went on. "And I ran into somebody I knew. Somebody from the city."

"You mean, someone from the—the gang?" Trixie asked.

Dan nodded. "Sort of. An older guy named Al Finlay. Lots of the gang members used to hang around with him. He's a real rat." Dan's hand clenched as he spoke. "It's a good thing Regan got me out of that gang before I was in too deep."

"We're all glad for that, Dan," Trixie said. "You must have thought this man Finlay had something to do with the arson attempt. That's why you kept asking us if anyone got a close look at the man in the garden."

Dan nodded. "Among other things, Al Finlay is a firebug. He said he was just passing through when I bumped into him in town. But when you told me about the arson attempt, I couldn't help thinking he was involved. Arson is just one of his ways of forcing people to do something they don't want to do." Dan nodded toward the pump. "Sabotage is another way."

"But why Mrs. Elliot?" Trixie asked. "What has she got that he would be interested in?"

"The only thing Al Finlay's interested in is money," Dan said.

Trixie was confused. "If that's so, and he stole the Social Security checks, then why did he throw them away?"

Dan shrugged.

"What about hidden money?" Trixie asked. "Maybe Mr. Elliot *did* hide some money here, and Finlay is trying to find it."

"Why burn down a building where the money might be hidden?" Dan countered.

Trixie had no answer for that.

Gravel crunched in the drive as the Elliots'

pickup pulled in. Max Elliot got out of the cab and walked around to the back to open the tailgate.

"Do you think Max has *something* to do with it?" Trixie asked Dan quietly.

Dan squinted. "Bad things didn't start happening around here until Max came back from the city," he said. "I'll help him unload the new pump. Don't say anything about this."

Trixie pointed to the suction pipe. "What about the hole? If the new pump is hooked up, it'll be ruined, too."

"Not for several hours," said Dan. "Max will want to make sure that it's drawing water. Let's let him discover the sabotage. Maybe we'll learn something."

Mart and Honey were approaching from the garden. Mrs. Elliot and Bobby came out onto the porch, carrying trays of lemonade and cookies.

Max frowned and asked, "What is this, a party? What are we celebrating?"

"We came to take some pictures," Trixie explained. "Pictures of your flowers to enter in a contest in the White Plains newspaper."

"I'm just their driver," Dan said good-naturedly. "I figured as long as I was here, I could help you install the new pump."

Max eyed the four Bob-Whites for a moment and then shrugged. "Okay. So help, already."

While Max and Dan unloaded the pump, the others helped set out refreshments on the picnic table behind the cottage.

Bobby snatched a cookie and said, "I'll help 'stall the new pump, too."

"You keep out of the way," Trixie advised, but Bobby was already running toward the well.

Max and Dan were carrying the pump between them on a length of board. Bobby dashed between them, ducking under it.

"Hey! Watch it!" Dan shouted.

Bobby tripped on the horizontal suction pipe and sprawled on the soft ground beyond the well. Max and Dan set the pump down and hurried to see if Bobby was hurt. Trixie and Honey rushed up behind.

"I'm not hurt," Bobby assured them, wiping dirt from his face. "But my cookie is broken!"

"Your cookie is dirty, too," Trixie said, brushing him off and giving him a hug. "And so are you. We'll get you another cookie and get you cleaned up a bit. You did manage to stay clean for quite a while."

"I hope he didn't damage that pipe," Dan said, noting that the suction pipe had been moved slightly by the impact of Bobby's foot.

"No, it swivels back and forth on its mounting," Max said, kneeling. "See? I'll just pull it—" He stopped suddenly, and his face reddened. He fingered the bottom of the pipe for a moment, then hunched down low to examine it. Max turned and looked from person to person, stopping at Dan. "There's a hole in the pipe," he said flatly.

"I didn't mean to break it!" Bobby wailed. "I'm sorry!"

"You didn't break it," Max said, not taking his eyes off Dan. "It looks like somebody cut a hole in it." The two young men stared at one another for a moment. "You knew about this, didn't you?" Max asked Dan. "Why didn't you say something? The new pump would have been ruined, too."

"I discovered it just before you got here," Dan admitted. "I thought maybe it would be better if you found it yourself."

"Oh, dear," Mrs. Elliot said in a worried tone. "More vandalism. Will the whole pipe have to be replaced?"

"No," Dan assured her. "Just that horizontal length. In the meantime, we should be able to patch that up." He kneeled beside Max. "Have you got an old piece of inner tube and a couple of hose clamps?" he asked.

Max nodded. "In the shed. I'll be right back."

When Max was out of sight, Mrs. Elliot sighed. "I'm sorry for the way Max has been acting," she said. "Things haven't gone too well since he came back from the city, and he can't help but feel that somehow he's to blame."

"That's all right; we understand," Trixie assured her.

"I'd like to think that someday this farm will be his," Mrs. Elliot went on, "but—"

116

"That won't be for a long, long time," Honey interrupted.

"Thank you, dear," Mrs. Elliot said.

Trixie was curious. "You make it sound like Max won't be here. Do you think he's going to, uh, leave again?"

"Oh, nothing like that," Mrs. Elliot said. She shook her head. "It's just that, well . . . he doesn't seem to want to own the place. I offered to have the deed put in his name now, but he refused. I offered him co-ownership, too, but he didn't want any part of that, either."

Before Trixie could say anything, Max returned with the mending materials. "This'll just take a few minutes," Dan told the others. "Go ahead and have some lemonade. Max and I will join you when we're done."

"I'll help Bobby get cleaned up first," Honey said, taking his hand.

"And I'm going to put the camera in the car," Mart added, "so he doesn't trip over *that!*"

While they were pouring tall glasses of iced lemonade, Trixie asked Mrs. Elliot, "Have other bad things happened recently? Have there

117

been other acts of vandalism?"

"Yes." Mrs. Elliot nodded. "I just can't understand it. It's so cruel and senseless. And it's happened so often, it's almost as if someone purposely. . . ." Her voice trailed off.

"What sort of things?" Trixie asked.

"My bed of snapdragons, for instance." Mrs. Elliot smiled wanly. "Isn't that a fierce name for such a beautiful flower?"

Trixie nodded. Mrs. Elliot went on. "Manton's, the flower shop in White Plains, ordered several dozen of them recently. I had an extra nice batch coming along. On the morning I was to cut and deliver them, someone had romped through them, trampling almost all of them down."

"Oh, no!" Trixie exclaimed. "Did you see any footprints? Could it have been a dog or a deer?"

"There was no way to tell. Max and I tried to find any flowers that could be saved, but there weren't enough. I'd been counting on the sale of those flowers."

Trixie frowned. "Were there other things, too? Other suspicious 'accidents'?"

"I'm afraid so," Mrs. Elliot said. "A few weeks ago, Max and I took a delivery to White Plains. When we came back to the truck after doing a little shopping, one of the tires had been slashed. The service station man couldn't repair it. I had to buy a new tire."

"Mrs. Elliot," Honey called from the porch. "There's a telephone call for you."

"Excuse me, dear," Mrs. Elliot told Trixie. "Why don't you take Max and Dan a glass of lemonade? I'll be right back."

Honey and Bobby joined her as Trixie put two glasses of lemonade and several cookies on a tray.

"Here's another cookie for you," Honey told Bobby affectionately.

"Don't go falling on that one," Trixie warned him with a smile. She took the tray to the well.

The suction pipe had been patched, and the new pump was hooked up. Max and Dan wiped their hands on paper napkins and paused for refreshing gulps of lemonade.

"Will it work?" Trixie asked, nodding toward the pump.

"Only one way to find out," Dan said. He set down his empty glass and kneeled to unscrew the priming plug. Max inserted a funnel and poured in a pail of water, priming the pump.

When the plug was tightened back into place, Max flipped the switch while Dan opened a nearby faucet. The motor hummed, and after a moment there was a brief spurt of water from the faucet. Then there were sputtering sounds as air came out of the tap, and a few more spurts of water. Finally there came a steady, gushing stream.

Everyone cheered, then headed for the picnic table for more refreshments.

Mrs. Elliot returned from the cottage beaming with pleasure. "That was Manton's, the flower shop, on the phone. Mr. Manton wanted to know if I could sell him a large quantity of red and white carnations. And I've got dozens of them that will be just right by next Tuesday."

"That's wonderful!" Honey said. The others agreed.

As more lemonade and cookies were consumed, Trixie pondered what Mrs. Elliot had told her. All of Mrs. Elliot's bad luck seemed to have started after Max came back from the city. But there was nothing to link Max to any of the troubles . . . and no real reason to suspect him.

"At least your Social Security check wasn't stolen," Trixie muttered.

"What, dear?" Mrs. Elliot inquired, overhearing. "Oh, yes. It *is* a good thing that I had them start sending the checks directly to the bank."

"How long ago did you start?" Trixie asked.

"My last check was the first one to be delivered that way," Mrs. Elliot said with a self-satisfied chuckle.

"Oh!" Trixie gasped. Maybe she was onto something. "What made you decide to do it?"

"Max suggested it," Mrs. Elliot said proudly.

Trixie almost dropped her glass of lemonade. She realized that Max was glowering at her. He had overheard the conversation, and he had to realize that Trixie suspected him of something. Trixie glanced nervously at Dan, who raised his eyebrows questioningly.

"Thanks a lot," Max said curtly. "For your

121

help, I mean. I've got work to do now." He stalked away.

Trixie blushed and put her glass down. "Thanks very much for the refreshments, Mrs. Elliot," she said. "I think it's time we went home."

Trixie Finds a Link • 7

MART's PHOTOGRAPHS of the sweet peas were all very good, and Trixie and Honey agonized over the selection of one print to enter in the photo contest. They planned to submit the entry in person, since Miss Trask was driving them to White Plains to pick up Brian and Jim. The bus bringing the young men home from camp would arrive in White Plains in the early afternoon.

"This'll be a lot faster than mailing in the

entry," Trixie said optimistically, climbing into the B.W.G. station wagon with Honey and Mart. "Maybe it'll get into this week's contest. The sooner the better for Mrs. Elliot."

Miss Trask slid in behind the steering wheel. "I don't like to dampen your enthusiasm, Trixie," she said, "but there must be hundreds of entries. I hope you haven't led Mrs. Elliot to believe she can definitely count on some prize money."

"Mrs. Elliot is more sagacious about it than Trixie," Mart commented. To Trixie he said, "That means she's got more *s-e-n-s-e*."

"She could use a whole lot of the other kind of cents," Trixie retorted. "Besides, don't you think your photograph is good enough to win the contest?"

"Ow!" Mart winced.

"Touché," said Miss Trask with a grin.

After delivering the photograph and entry blank to the White Plains newspaper office, Miss Trask and the three Bob-Whites drove to a nearby shopping center, where the camp bus would be unloading in the parking lot.

"We have nearly an hour until the bus is due," Miss Trask said, glancing at her wristwatch. "Plenty of time to do a little shopping. Shall we stick together or split up?"

"I'm not in the mood for earrings and purses," Mart said, wrinkling his nose. "I'm headed for the sporting goods store. See you in about an hour."

"Trixie? Honey?" Miss Trask inquired.

"We'll meet you here in an hour, too," Trixie said, "if it's all right with you."

"Fine," Miss Trask said. She headed for a department store.

Honey eyed Trixie, curious. "What are *we* going to shop for?" she asked.

"Flowers," Trixie said. "At Manton's Flower Shop. Come on."

As they left the parking lot and headed up the sidewalk, Honey asked, "What are we looking for at Manton's?"

"A link," Trixie said. "A connection of some kind. All of the bad things that have happened to Mrs. Elliot are somehow connected with her flower business. The arson attempt, the water

125

pump sabotage, the trampled bed of snap-dragons—"

Honey interrupted. "What about the slashed tire? And the attempt to steal her Social Security check?"

"The tire got slashed while she was here in White Plains delivering flowers to Manton's," Trixie pointed out. "And if her check *had* been stolen, she wouldn't have been able to get a new pump. She'd be out of business."

Honey nodded. "You're right. But what are we going to find at Manton's?"

"I don't know," Trixie admitted. "I'll just put my nose in a few flowers and see what I smell."

"I hope you don't get stung by a bee," Honey said in a half-serious tone.

"I've been thinking about those stolen checks," Trixie went on. "Maybe whoever stole them threw them away on purpose."

"What?" Honey asked.

"Maybe he wasn't interested in any of the checks except Mrs. Elliot's. Maybe he stole all the others to make it look like he wasn't after just hers."

126

Honey raised her eyebrows. "That's why, when he didn't find Mrs. Elliot's check, he didn't bother to steal any more on Glen Road. Right?"

"Right," Trixie affirmed. "And that's why he threw the other checks away."

Trixie and Honey had walked several blocks from the shopping center. The flower shop wasn't in the newest part of town; it was in a run-down area, on a side street. Tall buildings across from it prevented the sun from reaching the dirty windows. The only brightness in the neighborhood was the display of flowers Trixie and Honey could see in the window of the small shop.

Trixie opened the door. A chime sounded softly, and the cloying odor of flowers wrapped itself around the girls.

"I prefer the smell of flowers in a garden outside," Trixie murmured to Honey.

"The fragrance is too strong in a small room," Honey agreed.

Potted plants and a variety of vases cluttered the small shop. There was a desk with thick ring binders illustrating special displays to be ordered by number. Along one wall was a glass-doored cooler containing bundles of fresh flowers.

An open door at the back of the shop revealed a tiny office. Inside, a dark-haired man was turning the pages of a ledger. He looked up briefly, then dropped his eyes back to the ledger.

A tall, redheaded young woman in a green smock was working on a flower arrangement at a table near another open door, which led to the parking lot behind the building. She wiped her stained hands on her smock and stepped forward.

"Good afternoon," she said wearily. "May I help. . . . Well! Hi, Trixie! Hi, Honey!"

Trixie stared, trying to recognize her.

"I'm Ann Rinehart," the girl said. "My sister Debbie was in school with you until we moved here from Sleepyside."

"I remember now," Trixie said. "Hi!"

Honey smiled and nodded. "How do you and Debbie like living in White Plains?"

The young woman frowned. "Not much. Living in the city is a hassle. But, you know how—"

The dark-haired man came out from the office. "I'll take care of these young ladies," he said curtly. "Get back to work on that arrangement you were making."

He smiled, but the smile looked like a cardboard cutout pasted on his face. His shining dark eyes looked like circles of one-way glass. Trixie felt a chill wriggle along her spine.

"What may I do for you?" the man prompted.

"We were just looking," Honey said.

"For anything in particular?" the man asked impatiently. "Potted flowers or cut? A display for local delivery, or something ordered by wire?"

Trixie glanced about nervously, seeking an answer for his questions. Her eyes focused out the back door, and she saw the front of a car parked there—a *gray* car!

"Th-That's right," Trixie stammered. "We were just looking, Mr. Finlay."

The man's expression didn't change. "Where did you get that name? Mine's Manton."

"Oh, I'm sorry." Trixie gulped. "I—I guess we have the wrong shop."

Honey nodded jerkily.

"I don't know anybody in the flower business named Finlay," the man said. He raised his voice without taking his eyes off Trixie and Honey. "Let that flower arrangement go for now," he called to his redheaded helper. "Take your coffee break."

Without looking up, Ann Rinehart pulled off her smock, grabbed her purse, and hurried out the back door.

The man stepped to one side and gestured toward the office. "Get in there. We'll see if the name you want is in the phone book."

The door chime knelled softly. Trixie turned and saw Mart. *Saved by the bell!* she thought with relief.

"We got the wrong flower shop, Mart!" she exclaimed loudly. "Are all the others waiting in the car? Come on, Honey, we'll have to scout around town. Maybe we've got the wrong town! Thanks for your offer to help, Mr. Manton."

Mart picked up his cue. "I didn't think this

was the right place," he said. He opened the door. "Let's go."

Trixie and Honey hurried out of the shop. Walking rapidly toward the corner, Trixie resisted the urge to look back.

"You came just in time," she told Mart. "But how—"

"I saw you two go off by yourselves," Mart said. "Since you weren't staying with Miss Trask, I figured you were up to something. I just followed you."

"This is one time I'm glad you did," Trixie admitted.

"I was watching through the window," Mart said. "It looked like you wanted out of there in a hurry. What was going on?"

"I think he's the man who tried to set the fire," Trixie said. "There was a gray car parked out back. Maybe we ought to go around the block and take a look at it."

"Are you kidding?" Mart asked. "After that little act back there? Besides, I'm supposed to be keeping your wild geese under control, remember?"

"The day of the arson attempt," Trixie declared, "a gray car was backed into the bushes and against a small tree."

"So maybe there are some scratches on it," Mart said. "That doesn't prove anything. Most cars have scratches and nicks."

"I don't think that man is a florist at all," Trixie stated. "His hands weren't stained green like Ann's were."

"I noticed that, too," Honey said. "He was going over the books. It looked like Ann was doing all the real work."

Trixie nodded agreement. "And he wasn't the least bit interested in us until he heard Debbie's sister mention Sleepyside."

"Then he dropped what he was doing and came out of the office," Honey said. "The way he looked at us!"

As they approached the shopping center parking lot, the B.W.G.'s saw the camp bus unloading. A cheerful crowd of adults and young people exchanged greetings.

"Don't you dare say anything about this to Miss Trask," Trixie warned Mart. "Honey and

I will bring the other Bob-Whites up to date
later on."

During the ride back to Sleepyside, Jim and
Brian told about their two weeks at the camp
for underprivileged children. Brian, in addition
to being a tent leader, had assisted in the doctor's tent, where he helped treat cuts, poison
ivy, and stomachaches.

"There weren't many serious medical problems," Brian said. "But we did have one near-
drowning. Luckily, Jim got to the boy as he
was going under for the third time. And Jim
revived him with mouth-to-mouth resuscita-
tion. He's the camp hero!"

Everyone in the B.W.G. station wagon
cheered, even Miss Trask.

Jim was embarrassed. "He was swimming
when he shouldn't have been. It's a tough way
to learn a lesson, but he learned. A couple of
other boys in my tent admitted that they had
been planning some extra swimming, too. They
changed their minds pretty fast. What's been
happening around here . . . anything?"

Mart winced. Trixie eyed him sternly, then began telling Jim and Brian about happenings of the last two weeks. She told about Dan discovering the sabotaged water pump, but didn't mention the man named Al Finlay.

"That's about all," Trixie concluded. "Now that you're back, we can have a meeting at the clubhouse tomorrow. If I think of anything else, I can tell everyone about it then."

The following morning, after completing their chores, Trixie, Brian, and Mart walked to the B.W.G. clubhouse on the Wheeler estate. Honey, Jim, and Di met them there.

Honey motioned Trixie aside and whispered, "Dan couldn't make it to the meeting today. I talked to him last night. I didn't mention the flower shop, but I asked him to describe Al Finlay—just in case we should happen to see him."

"Well?" Trixie prompted.

"It was him. The man in the flower shop," Honey confirmed.

"I thought so," Trixie said.

Jim spoke up from behind. "I got the impression that you were holding back something yesterday," he said. "What's up?"

"They think they've found the man who's been making problems for Mrs. Elliot," Mart said. "And I think maybe they're on the right track."

Trixie gaped at the unexpected support from her brother. She told the others about Al Finlay, and then described what had happened at the flower shop. "I tried the name Finlay on him, but he didn't show any reaction," she said.

"Not right then," Honey joined in. "But right after that, he told Ann to take a break. I don't know what he would have done to us if Mart hadn't come in."

Jim shook his head. "I don't like this. It's too dangerous. If that man really is Al Finlay, then he must have a police record. I say we call Sergeant Molinson."

Trixie moaned. "He'll just say we don't have any proof."

"You don't," Brian pointed out.

"Well, then, what can Sergeant Molinson do?" Trixie retorted. "He can't just arrest Finlay for no reason."

"Maybe the police already want him for some other crime," Mart suggested.

"But if they arrest him for some other crime," Honey said, "then he won't be punished for what he's tried to do to Mrs. Elliot."

"And we'll never know *why* he tried to do it," Trixie added.

Brian nodded. "I suppose you have a plan. Right, Trixie?"

"Yes, I do," Trixie said. "Honey and I are going to have a slumber party."

The other Bob-Whites—including Honey— looked at one another in surprised silence. "A slumber party?" Brian repeated.

Trixie nodded. "Monday night. Honey is going to invite Di and me to spend the night at her place. And you, Brian, are going to invite Jim to spend the night at our house."

"And what are we going to do in our soporific state?" Mart asked sarcastically. "Dream of capturing Al Finlay?"

"We're not going to sleep at all, if that's what you mean," Trixie said. "At midnight, we're all going to meet right here at the clubhouse."

"You mean sneak out of the houses?" Di asked nervously.

"We'll have to," Trixie said in a serious tone. "It's the only way we will be able to stand guard at Mrs. Elliot's."

"I don't get it," Jim said.

"The last time Mrs. Elliot had a big order of flowers to sell," Trixie explained, "they were trampled down on the night before she was to pick them."

"The snapdragons," Honey said.

"That's right," Trixie said. "Now she has a big order for carnations. She's going to pick and deliver them on Tuesday morning. So, on Monday night, we're going to stand guard over the carnations."

"That sure won't be a bed of roses," Mart quipped.

"No, it won't," Brian agreed. "If we get caught sneaking out of the house at night, we may be grounded for the whole summer."

"Well, somebody has got to guard those flowers," Trixie said stubbornly. "I'll do it myself if I have to."

"Hold on," Jim cautioned. "If we do anything, we'll do it together. That's what the Bob-Whites are all about. Let's just make sure we know what we may be getting into."

"Besides Max," Trixie said, "we're the only ones who know that Mrs. Elliot has that flower order."

"You don't suspect Max, do you?" Di asked.

Trixie shook her head. "Not directly. I think maybe he knows something about what's been happening, but he won't say. The only other person who knows about the flower order is Finlay, alias Manton. If he's the one who's trying to ruin Mrs. Elliot's flower business, then he may try something on Monday night."

Di looked worried. "Couldn't we just tell Sergeant Molinson to put a stakeoff—"

"You mean a stake*out*," Mart corrected.

"A stakeout," Di went on, "at Mrs. Elliot's on Monday night?"

Jim shook his head. "He'd want some kind of proof that something was going to happen to the flowers."

"We'd have to reveal our whole plan," Trixie

added, "and Molinson would tell our parents, and they would tell us that we were jumping to conclusions, and—"

"And nobody would guard the flowers," Di concluded.

Mart shrugged. "Why all the syllogistics? Trixie's already made up our minds for us."

Jim sighed. "Mart's right. But we should take a vote to make it official. Remember: This could be dangerous. And if our folks find out about it, we could be in big trouble. All in favor of Trixie's plan raise your hand."

Trixie's hand went up, then Mart's and Brian's. Honey looked at Jim, and when he raised his hand, she raised hers. Di swallowed and raised her hand, too.

"It's unanimous," Jim said. "Now, let's agree on something else. We'll need the B.W.G. station wagon to get to Mrs. Elliot's. Once we're there, we'll stick close to the wagon. If we see something happening, we won't try to stop it ourselves—we'll head for the police, fast. Okay?"

The others nodded.

"Any questions?" Jim asked.

Mart raised his hand. "I have a question. Why couldn't my sister be interested in something safe and sensible . . . like hockey or professional wrestling?"

Night Watch • 8

THE MOON PEEKED between tree branches, covering the damp ground with a patchwork of cold light. Trixie hunched her shoulders and pushed her hands deep into the pockets of her jacket. Di, standing beside her, shivered.

"Cold?" Trixie asked.

"Scared," Di admitted. "I've been rearranging all of my goose bumps."

"If you need any more," said Honey, "I've got plenty to spare."

Jim jingled the keys to the station wagon. "There's no need for all of us to go over there," he said. "Brian, Mart, and I could go."

"Oh, sure," Trixie protested. "This was my idea, and now you want to leave me out of it."

"You wouldn't be out of it," Brian said. "We'd leave one of these with you." He patted a leather case attached to his belt. It contained a walkie-talkie, one of a set given to Mart the previous Christmas. "One of us will keep you informed of what's going on, if anything."

Trixie shook her head. "You're not leaving me behind. We need both walkie-talkies at Mrs. Elliot's. One of us has to stay in the car in case we need to get away fast. Whoever that is will need a walkie-talkie to be alerted. The other walkie-talkie has to be where we're keeping watch."

"And another thing," Honey pointed out. "Leaving us behind would be a form of sex discrimination."

"Gee," said Mart, "I should have thought of that before I held the door open for you at Manton's Flower Shop."

142

"Maybe we ought to equalize the situation," Jim said. "We'll stay here and let them go." He tossed the keys to Trixie.

"But I can't drive," Trixie said.

"That puts it on us," Brian said to Jim. "I'd call that age discrimination, wouldn't you?"

"There's only one way to settle this," Honey said with a nervous giggle. "We'll all go."

"I knew it all along," Jim admitted. He retrieved the keys from Trixie. "Let's get started, or it'll be daylight by the time we get to Mrs. Elliot's."

It was decided that Jim would stay in the station wagon when they arrived. The others would spread out in different directions, keeping as close to the wagon as possible.

"There is one essential facet of this operation that has been overlooked," Mart commented.

"Such as?" Trixie prompted.

"Just *where* is the bed of carnations whose slumber we're supposed to sentinel?"

"That's right," Jim said. "I hadn't thought of that."

"Uh-oh!" Trixie pursed her lips. "I know

143

where the sweet peas are, and the delphiniums, and clematis, and roses—"

"The carnations?" Mart urged.

Brian looked at Trixie. "Are we going to have to go searching around in the dark?"

"Tiptoeing through the tulips?" Mart added.

"Tulips are not in season," Trixie snapped.

"I know where the carnations are," Honey said. "I remember seeing them on the afternoon the new pump was put in."

"Tell us as exactly as you can," Jim said. "You don't want to make noise blundering around, and it would be better if no one has to use a flashlight."

Honey described having seen the carnations beyond the shed, to one side of the cornfield. "They're in a big open area where the corn won't shade them," she said.

Trixie nodded. "Now I remember. I saw them there on the day of the arson attempt. The carnations just didn't register with me. I had other things on my mind."

"As usual," Mart said.

Brian spoke up. "That location solves a problem. We won't have to go past the house and chance alarming Mrs. Elliot."

"Brian's right," Jim said. "We don't have to use Mrs. Elliot's drive. We'll go up the lane on the other side of the cornfield, where the gray car was."

"If someone does come," Honey warned, "he might use that same road."

"We'll spot him that much sooner if he does," Jim said. "I'll have the wagon hidden off to the side."

Trixie leaned forward. "Brian, you and Di take the far side of the clearing, opposite the cornfield. There are some bushes there to hide in. Mart," she continued, turning to him, "you take the front of the clearing. Honey and I will cut through the corn to the near side."

"If you get hungry," Mart said, "you can munch on an ear of corn."

Di spoke up, trying to sound braver than she felt. "Just be sure it isn't popcorn. Too noisy."

Jim turned the B.W.G. station wagon off Glen Road and onto the rough lane that led around behind Mrs. Elliot's property.

"Drive slowly," Brian cautioned. "We don't want to make too much noise."

"Can you see without the headlights on?" Trixie asked.

Jim switched the headlights off. "I can see well enough," he said. "We're almost there." A moment later, he pulled off the lane. "Here we are," he said in a hushed tone. He turned the engine off.

The young people sat for a moment in the stillness surrounding the station wagon. Trixie still had her hands thrust deep into the pockets of her jacket. She was glad she'd worn it— though it didn't seem to be keeping her very warm at the moment. She pulled a hand free and reached for the door handle. "I guess we'd better . . . get into position," she whispered.

"Keep it quiet," Jim advised. "Don't slam the doors. I'll turn the wagon around so that we can pull out fast if we have to."

In the pale moonlight, their faces looked ghostly white. "See you later," Trixie said. She kept herself from adding, "I hope."

"Good luck," said Jim. "You'd better not use

the flashlights if you can avoid it."

"Sure," Mart said, "just use your scotopic vision."

Trixie and Honey crossed the lane. The tall corn reared up in the darkness like a solid wall. Trixie reached out and spread two stalks so she could step between them.

"Hope we don't get lost in here," Honey murmured behind her.

"We'll have to sort of feel the furrows with our feet," Trixie said softly. "We'll keep going across them. Don't follow me too closely—maybe you can keep me going in a straight line."

Trixie parted another pair of stalks. They rustled dryly, sounding awfully loud in the darkness. A rough corn leaf rasped across her cheek.

A sudden shrill squeak and a flutter of motion made Trixie cringe back. A small bird scolded indignantly and flew off.

Both girls stood for a moment, breathing hard.

"At least," Honey gasped, "it wasn't a snake."

Trixie tensed. There would be snakes in here

147

—corn snakes, garter snakes, maybe even poisonous copperheads or rattlers. She gritted her teeth and gingerly put a foot forward in the darkness. Now she wished she'd worn boots instead of sneakers.

The girls moved on slowly across the dark cornfield. After a few minutes, Honey called out softly, "Trixie!"

Trixie turned but couldn't see Honey. "Where are you? What is it?"

"Come straight back. I'm stuck."

Trixie backtracked a few paces until Honey's ghostly face appeared.

"My hair's caught," Honey said. "I can't get it free." She spoke apologetically. "I should have put it up."

"We should have done a lot of things differently," Trixie agreed. Honey's hair was caught on a tall weed of some kind. Trixie couldn't unsnag it without breaking the plant, which made more noise than she would have liked.

"We must be about in the center of the cornfield now," Trixie whispered. "I hope we've been going straight."

Trixie parted two stalks but paused before stepping between them. In moving around to untangle Honey's hair, she had lost her sense of direction. Now she didn't know which way to go.

"Do you know which way we should go?" she asked Honey.

"That way." Honey pointed. "I think. I got turned around trying to free my hair. . . ."

Trixie sighed. "We'll have to use the flashlight to get our bearings. Shield it with your hand."

The light shining through Honey's palm made the hand look reddish and bony.

"Point it at the ground and let a little more light out," Trixie said. "If we can find our footprints, then we'll know which way to go."

As Honey directed the light downward, a pair of beady little eyes gleamed redly nearby. Honey gasped and covered the light again. There was a rasping sound of tiny feet scurrying away in the dry litter on the ground.

"What was that?" Honey whispered shakily.

"A field mouse," Trixie said. Her toes curled

in her sneakers. "Let out some light again."

As Honey moved the beam of light around, they found a line of footprints. "Those are mine," said Trixie. "Where I came back to help you."

"Then," said Honey, moving the light to the other side, "that's the direction we should go." She snapped off the light. "I've heard about people being lost for days in cornfields in the Midwest."

"This cornfield isn't that big," Trixie said. She frowned in the darkness. "Turn the light on again. Keep it down." She looked at the stalks surrounding them. "Raise the light a little. Carefully."

She saw many small green leaves and twigs. "That's not corn!" Trixie exclaimed.

"What is it?"

"I don't know. Move the light around."

As far as they could see, the tall green plants were all the same. They definitely weren't corn plants.

"I don't know what these are," Trixie repeated, "but I'll bet Max does."

"Yes," Honey breathed. "Max was working here with a hoe on the day of the arson attempt. I thought that the corn where he was standing seemed different from that in the rest of the field. I was about to mention it when you spotted the man with the gasoline can at the shed."

Trixie nodded in the darkness. "Max was standing in these plants, whatever they are. I wonder if they have anything to do with what's been happening here. Maybe Max is involved, after all."

"But Max couldn't be involved," Honey said. "He was the one who saved Mrs. Elliot's Social Security check by having her mail it to the bank."

"Yes," Trixie agreed. "But still, Mrs. Elliot didn't have any problems until Max came back from the city. There must be some connection."

"I wonder what these plants have to do with everything," Honey mused. "This keeps getting more and more confusing."

"It sure does," Trixie said. "Let's take some pieces of these plants along with us. We'll ask

Mart if he knows what they are."

"They're probably just weeds," Honey said.

"Then why didn't Max hoe them down?" Trixie asked. She broke off stems and leaves and thrust them into her jacket pockets. Then she led the way toward the clearing. After a moment, something scraped against Trixie's head. She reached up and felt a large leaf of corn.

They came to the edge of the cornfield and paused to get their bearings. The well and water pump were off to the left in the darkness. The cottage was beyond, with one shaded window glowing with soft light. Somewhere ahead, in the darkness, should be the clearing for the carnations.

Trixie wondered if the others had reached their positions. She pursed her lips and gave the Bob-White whistle, very softly. There was no response.

The girls moved quietly ahead, stepping slowly, feeling first to make sure there were no twigs underfoot to snap.

Trixie placed her right foot ahead and felt something soft and squirmy under it—a snake!

152

She choked off a scream and jumped back in alarm, knocking into Honey.

Honey gasped, clutching her. "What's the matter?" She whispered in a painful tone, "You stepped on my toes."

"I stepped on a *snake* . . . I think."

Honey shuddered. "Did it bite you?"

"I don't think so. I didn't feel anything."

"Is it still there?" Honey asked in a shaky whisper. "We'd better make sure with the flashlight." She handed the light to Trixie. "You look. I can't."

Trixie covered the flashlight with her hand and switched it on. She stared sheepishly at the length of garden hose stretched snakelike across the path.

Honey peeked, then giggled softly. "I would have panicked, too," she admitted. "What are you waiting for?"

Trixie swallowed hard. "Just trying to get my heart back down where it belongs."

Trembling with excitement, the girls moved ahead once more. As they passed some deeply shadowed bushes, there was a rustle, and a figure of a man appeared. Trixie gasped, and Honey swung the darkened flashlight. It struck solidly.

"Hey!" Mart exclaimed. He lowered his voice to an angry whisper. "Are you trying to break my wrist? What's the matter with you two? Where have you been? What took you so long?"

"Shh!" Trixie cautioned.

But it was too late. Light flooded the garden from a spotlight under the cottage eaves. The door opened, and Max came out with a powerful flashlight in one hand and a piece of metal pipe in the other.

"What are *you* doing here?" he demanded.

Mrs. Elliot appeared behind him, wearing a long, quilted robe. "Goodness!" she exclaimed. "It's Trixie and Honey. I was going to call the police. It's after midnight."

Max directed the blinding light at the three startled faces, moving it back and forth from one to the other.

"What are you doing here?" he demanded again.

Trixie found her voice and directed it past

him to Mrs. Elliot. "We're sorry we frightened you, Mrs. Elliot. We didn't mean any harm. We—we knew you had an order of flowers for tomorrow, and the last time, someone trampled them all down on the night before. We thought we'd just sort of quietly stand guard over the carnations."

Mrs. Elliot shook her head. "That was thoughtful of you, but—"

"Oh, yeah," Max interrupted. "Maybe they came to trample the carnations themselves!"

Before Trixie could reply, she heard feet hurrying through the garden from the other lane. Brian and Di came into the area of light.

Brian looked apologetically at Mrs. Elliot. "We're sorry. We only came to—"

"Trixie has already explained," Mrs. Elliot said.

Trixie felt a nudge from Honey. Honey's gaze lowered pointedly to Trixie's jacket pocket. Some of the leaves of the strange plant poked out. Trixie thrust them down out of sight.

Mrs. Elliot continued. "It was kind of you to plan on staying out all night to protect my flowers, but it wasn't necessary. Show them, Max."

He pointed the powerful flashlight into the nearby clearing. The young people saw a mass of pale green plants, but no carnations on them.

"We picked them late this afternoon," Mrs. Elliot said, "and placed them in the cooler in wet moss. They'll be ready for delivery first thing in the morning."

"Oh!" Trixie gave the others an abashed, sheepish look.

Max spotlighted Trixie with the flashlight. "Disappointed?" he asked.

"Max!" Mrs. Elliot scolded. "These young people certainly didn't mean any harm. They were just trying to help."

Max stared at Trixie for a moment. "Yeah," he said. "Just trying to help." He switched off the flashlight.

Trixie swallowed. "Did you pick the carnations today because you were afraid that . . . something would happen to them?"

Mrs. Elliot shook her head. "I hadn't really given that a thought," she said. "We had plen-

156

ty of room in the cooler, and Max suggested that—"

"It was Max's idea?" Trixie asked.

"It was my idea," Max affirmed. "And, no, I didn't do it because I was afraid something would happen to the flowers. I just don't like to get up so early in the morning, that's all."

"You must be chilly," Mrs. Elliot said to the Bob-Whites. "Come in, and I'll make some hot chocolate."

"Thank you," Trixie said, "but we'd better be getting home." She turned to Mart. "Call Jim and have him come around here to pick us up." To Mrs. Elliot, she repeated, "We're really sorry to have frightened you. We were just trying to help."

"I know," Mrs. Elliot said. "You've been kind. I'm certainly glad that I didn't call the police."

Trixie winced. "So am I!" She couldn't imagine trying to explain this little outing to her parents *and* Sergeant Molinson.

Gravel crunched as the B.W.G. station wagon pulled into the drive. Jim got out and started to speak, but Honey interrupted him.

"We've already explained," she said. "Let's go, so Mrs. Elliot can get in out of the cold. Good night, Mrs. Elliot, Max."

Trixie, Brian, and Mart said sheepish goodnights and climbed into the wagon. Di was too embarrassed to say anything. On the way down Glen Road, Trixie explained to Jim what had happened.

"It *is* a good thing she didn't call the police," Jim said. "Being grounded is one thing, but being in jail. . . ."

"We aren't home free yet," Mart reminded him. "We still have to sneak into the houses without our folks catching us. If they hear us, maybe *they'll* call the police."

Trixie gulped.

Brian eyed Trixie and Honey. "The next time I let these two talk me into something like this, somebody kick me."

"We all voted on this," Jim said. "It seemed like a good idea at the time. Now I just want to get inside and go to bed and forget all about it."

Trixie slouched and tucked her hands into

her pockets. She felt the leaves and twigs inside. She started to speak but then changed her mind.

Better wait until tomorrow, she thought, *or they'll all kick* me.

A Strange Plant • 9

IN THE MORNING, the Bob-Whites met at the clubhouse for breakfast. The boys yawned and grumbled about lack of sleep, but Trixie, Honey, and Di were alert and cheerful.

"Why so Elysian this morning?" Mart inquired pompously.

"I don't know what that means," Trixie scoffed. "We're just relieved, that's all."

Honey nodded. "We didn't get caught."

"Not yet," Jim said. "What if Mrs. Elliot calls

our elders to tell them what wonderful kids we are?"

"Gleeps! I hadn't thought of that," Trixie admitted. "I wish we weren't so wonderful!"

Jim and Brian prepared bacon and scrambled eggs and lots of buttered toast. Their late-night adventure had given the young people hearty appetites.

After breakfast, Trixie removed a folded tissue from her pocket and opened it. The leaves inside were wilted, but still dark green.

"Does anybody know what this is?" Trixie asked.

"Where'd you find that?" Jim asked.

"In the cornfield last night," Trixie said. "There were lots of plants like this. They're surrounded by the corn."

"Sort of hidden," Honey said, "where we saw Max standing on the day of the arson attempt."

"I'm no botanist," Jim said, frowning.

"Neither am I," Brian agreed. His frown matched Jim's. "Hidden, you say? That suggests something."

"What?" Trixie inquired.

Brian shook his head. "Pass them down to Mart. Maybe he can tell for sure."

They turned. Mart was rubbing a swelling on his wrist where Honey had struck him with the flashlight.

"You're the future agriculturist," Trixie said, handing the tissue to Mart. "What kind of plant are these from?"

Mart was about to make a sarcastic remark, but his lips pressed closed and his gaze became intent. "What are you doing with that stuff?" he demanded.

"I just said that Honey and I found it at Mrs. Elliot's. What is it?"

Mart didn't answer. He took part of a leaf, crushed it in his palm, and smelled it. Next he broke a twig and smelled that also. "Do we have any matches here?" he asked.

Jim brought the matches from his camp stove. Mart struck one and burned a bit of one leaf.

"That smells like rope," Trixie said.

Mart nodded. "Because it's hemp." He looked intently at Trixie. "Have you got any more of

162

it? If you do, then get rid of it!"

"What *is* it?" Trixie insisted.

"I'm pretty sure it's *Cannabis*," Mart said seriously.

Brian spoke quietly. "I thought so, too. Especially since it was hidden in the cornfield."

"What on earth is *Cannabis?*" Honey asked.

"That's part of the scientific name," Mart said. "Usually it's just called marijuana."

"It's illegal!" Honey said. "So that's why Max is growing it hidden from sight."

"It might not be illegal for long," Jim said, frowning. "There are a lot of states considering legalizing it." He shook his head. "I'm not sure, but I think there's a bill in the New York legislature to legalize it."

"If it's going to be legal," Honey said, "then why hide where it's growing?"

"Because," Brian suggested, "if it was legal, there'd be regulations and taxes for producing and selling it, just like alcohol. If someone wanted to avoid those, he'd still hide the plants."

"That's why it's hidden in the middle of the

cornfield," Trixie said. "That's why Max didn't hoe it down."

"Mrs. Elliot's property is a good out-of-the-way place to grow something illegally," Honey added.

"And that's why," Trixie went on excitedly, "all those things are happening to Mrs. Elliot. She wouldn't allow anything illegal, of course, so they're trying to force her to give the place to Max."

"There's a problem with that theory," Jim said. "Max doesn't want the place. Remember what Mrs. Elliot told you? She offered to give the farm to him, but he refused. He didn't even want to be a co-owner."

"And," Honey said, "he's been doing things to protect Mrs. Elliot. *He* told her to have her Social Security check sent to the bank. *He* was the one who decided to pick the carnations earlier than usual."

"But why," asked Mart, "is he so huffy every time we suggest that something crooked is going on? He wants us to think that the things happening to Mrs. Elliot are just accidents."

"Check," Jim agreed. "I think he knows *none* of the things that have happened are accidents." Jim gestured to the leaves and twigs from the marijuana plant. "We're not sure whether Max is responsible for this or not. But we'd better inform Sergeant Molinson about it."

Trixie felt awful. "That'll mean *more* trouble for poor Mrs. Elliot. That stuff is growing on her property, and even if she doesn't know about it—"

"She couldn't," Honey said.

"Of course not," Trixie said. "But Sergeant Molinson will go over there to question Max." She closed her eyes and shook her head. "Mrs. Elliot really loves Max and wants him to get adjusted to the farm after living in the city."

"In the city," Brian repeated, "where he probably met Al Finlay. And now he's either brought Finlay here, or Finlay has followed him. . . . It's a mess for Mrs. Elliot, one way or the other."

"We'd better call Sergeant Molinson," Jim said again.

"Wait," Trixie said. "Maybe we should think

about getting some advice first."

"From whom?" Mart demanded.

"From Mr. Hartman. He's a good friend of Mrs. Elliot's, and he's also an ex-policeman."

Brian raised his eyebrows. "Can I believe what I'm hearing? You're admitting that you don't know what to do about this?"

"I didn't say that," Trixie retorted. "I just think we should be careful, for Mrs. Elliot's sake."

"Trixie's right," Honey said.

Di nodded agreement.

Jim ran a hand through his red hair. "I sure don't want to cause any more problems for Mrs. Elliot. But I don't want for us to get in trouble, either. If we *don't* tell Sergeant Molinson about the marijuana, and later on he finds out that we knew about it, he could arrest us for withholding evidence."

Mart whistled. "We'd have to change the Bob-White whistle to the jailbird whistle."

Honey paled. Di gulped.

"Getting some advice first is a good idea, though," Jim admitted. "And Mr. Hartman seems like the right person to ask."

Brian spoke up. "I don't know. Remember, Trixie, when we were at Mr. Hartman's asking about the Social Security checks? He hinted that he knew something suspicious about Mrs. Elliot's husband, Sam. But he wouldn't tell us what it was."

Trixie nodded. "He said it was over with. He didn't want Mrs. Elliot to find out about it, so he wouldn't talk about it."

"Whatever it was," Honey said, "may be starting all over again with Max. Maybe Mr. Hartman won't help us because it might hurt Mrs. Elliot."

"I guess we won't know until we ask," Trixie murmured.

After tidying up the clubhouse, the B.W.G.'s drove up Glen Road to the Hartmans'. They heard Mrs. Hartman's cane tapping toward the door as she came to answer their knock.

"Well, hello, Trixie . . . Brian." Mrs. Hartman smiled. "These must be the other young people you spoke about. How nice of you to come calling."

Trixie introduced the others. Then she asked, "Is Mr. Hartman here?"

"Oh, he left early this morning for a meeting of retired policemen," Mrs. Hartman said.

"When will he be back?" Trixie inquired.

"Not until the end of the week."

"That long?" Trixie exclaimed in dismay.

"Well, the meeting doesn't last that long." Mrs. Hartman smiled indulgently. "But ex-policemen are just like old soldiers or athletes when they get together. They've got to talk a lot and relive their times together. I suppose you're too young to know about that."

"Trixie knows about talking a lot," Mart commented.

Trixie gave him a sidelong look, then returned her attention to Mrs. Hartman. "We had a question to ask your husband. About Mrs. Elliot, sort of. I mean—"

"Oh, yes," Mrs. Hartman said. "Charles went over there yesterday, to ask them to keep an eye on me while he was gone."

"Of course," said Trixie. "He'd be concerned about your being here alone."

Mrs. Hartman nodded. "It's good he was there, too."

"Why?" Honey asked. "Did something happen?"

"Ethel had a phone call from a realty company saying they had a buyer for her place."

"Is she trying to sell it?" Trixie asked, surprise in her voice.

"Oh, my, no. Ethel loves that place. Evidently, though, someone else likes it, too, and asked the realty firm to make her an offer. She's had a bit of financial trouble recently—"

"We know," said Trixie, giving Honey a look.

"—so, naturally," Mrs. Hartman continued, "an offer to buy her place was tempting, much as she'd rather stay there. She asked Charles what he thought, and he told her the offer was much too low."

"What realty company was it?" Trixie inquired, curious.

"I don't know," Mrs. Hartman said.

Mrs. Hartman offered the young people doughnuts and milk, but they declined, explaining that they'd had a large breakfast. After a few minutes of visiting, the Bob-Whites excused themselves and piled back into the wagon.

"Let's go to Mrs. Elliot's," Trixie said.

"They won't be there," Jim reminded her. "They're delivering the carnations to Manton's this morning."

"I know," Trixie said, "but I want to look in that cornfield in the daylight."

Brian nodded. "That's a good idea."

As they were climbing out of the wagon in Mrs. Elliot's driveway, they heard the phone begin to ring in the cottage.

"I wonder who's calling," Trixie muttered.

"Whoever it is," Brian said after a moment, "is awfully anxious. I've counted fifteen rings. Ten rings are plenty before hanging up."

The phone stopped ringing on the twentieth ring.

The B.W.G.'s headed into the cornfield, pushing their way between the rows of corn. Suddenly they found themselves in a huge open space, surrounded by cornstalks.

Trixie groaned. "We're too late. It's already been harvested."

170

Jim walked ahead to a blackened heap in the middle of the open area.

"Harvested, nothing," he called back. He leaned close to the black mound and sniffed.

"Careful," Brian warned. "Don't breathe too much of that."

Jim stepped back. "I wasn't sniffing for the marijuana. I smelled something else. Gasoline." He poked his foot at blackened stalks, stems, and twigs. "That stuff was too green to burn without some help. Gasoline was poured on it."

"But why?" Di wanted to know.

"Because Trixie and I discovered it last night," Honey answered. "Trixie had it in her pockets. Some was sticking out, and I'm pretty sure Max saw it. He probably realized he'd have to get rid of it before we told the police."

"It doesn't make sense," Jim declared. "He and Finlay could have just cut it down and hidden it somewhere."

"Maybe they didn't think there was enough time for that," Brian suggested.

Trixie shook her head. "There was too much money involved in what was growing here. I don't think Finlay would have burned it up. And, in a way, this could still be evidence. So why leave it lying here like this?"

"Now what do we do, dear sister?" Brian asked.

Trixie scratched her head.

"Whatever we do," Di urged, "let's not do it here. I don't want to be seen anywhere near this stuff!"

"That's right," Honey said. "Let's get out of here and go somewhere where we can think."

Think, Trixie repeated silently. *For Mrs. Elliot's sake, think!*

A Confession · 10

As THE BOB-WHITES climbed out of the station wagon at Manor House, Regan and Dan came out of the garage, headed toward the stable.

"Well," Regan greeted them, "I was just about to run an ad in the paper for someone to exercise the horses. Help me, Dan—don't let them move in any direction except toward the stable."

Dan grinned and jumped to herd Trixie in the right direction. As he touched her arm, his grin vanished abruptly, and Trixie felt his grip tighten on her arm.

"What's the matter, Dan?" Trixie asked.

Glowering at her, Dan yanked her toward Honey and seized her arm, too. He raised it toward his face.

"Dan?" Honey asked in an alarmed tone.

"You crazy kids!" Dan snapped. "You've been smoking marijuana!"

"No!" they protested.

"Don't lie to me. I know the smell of it. I can smell it on all of you!"

Regan's face quickly flushed with anger, matching Dan's. The yard filled with the sound of accusations and protests.

The clamor brought Miss Trask hurrying from the house. The boys were shouting. Honey was crying. Trixie was on the verge of tears herself.

Miss Trask put her arm about Honey. "That's enough! All of you. What's this all about?"

"Can't you smell it?" Dan demanded. "They've been smoking marijuana!"

Miss Trask remained calm and kept her arm

around Honey. She looked squarely at Jim. "Well?" she asked.

"It's marijuana smoke you smell," Jim confirmed. "But we weren't smoking it. We were at Mrs. Elliot's this morning—"

"She and Max were gone," Trixie interrupted, hoping Jim would not mention their little "midnight mistake."

"We wanted to check something out," Jim went on. He described the smoldering mound they had discovered in the middle of the cornfield. "The smell of the smoke got into our clothes," he finished.

Regan nodded. "Marijuana. So that's what's been going on at Mrs. Elliot's place. Somehow I'm not surprised."

Dan shook his head. "I'm sorry. I should have realized I know you guys well enough to know you wouldn't try anything so dumb. That smell just—"

"It's all right, Dan," Honey sniffed.

"I'm sure Mrs. Elliot doesn't know about the marijuana," Trixie said. "But we saw Max in that very same spot on the day of the arson attempt at Mrs. Elliot's potting shed."

"That doesn't surprise me, either," Regan said. "Mrs. Elliot's troubles didn't seem to start until Max came back from the city. It all fits now."

"But Max—" Honey began.

Miss Trask spoke up. "Sergeant Molinson will have to be notified about this, as much as we'd like to save Mrs. Elliot from more distress. You discovered evidence of criminal activity, and it's your duty to report it."

"We know," Trixie admitted reluctantly.

"I'll phone him," Miss Trask said, turning toward the house.

While the others discussed the situation, Trixie motioned Dan aside. "I'm sure Al Finlay had something to do with this," she told him. "But why would he burn the marijuana?"

Dan shook his head. "I don't know. The police will still be able to identify it, even though it was burned."

"We thought so," Trixie said. "It's still evidence against whoever's responsible."

"Maybe," Dan said thoughtfully, "Finlay did

176

it to make more problems for Mrs. Elliot and Max. It's almost certain now that Max will end up in jail. That'll leave Mrs. Elliot without any help."

Trixie frowned. "I wish I could figure Max out. I'm sure he knows what's going on, but he won't say. Still, I'm not convinced that he has anything to do with it."

Sergeant Molinson's car squealed into the driveway. He climbed out and eyed the young people coldly. "Miss Trask said you had something very important to tell me—something about Max Elliot." He sniffed the air, and his frown deepened. "Did Max sell marijuana to you kids?" he growled.

"No," Jim said. "We're not even sure that Max is involved." He described once again the discovery in the cornfield. "We did see Max in approximately the same spot a couple weeks ago," Jim said. "But he could have—"

"It figures," Molinson said, jotting notes in his pad. He looked up at the Bob-Whites. "I might as well tell you that Max already has a police record."

177

"Are you sure?" Trixie asked.

Molinson turned red. "Young lady, I—" He paused and took a breath. "I'm sure because Max told me himself, after the arson attempt. When I took his fingerprints to compare them with those on the gasoline can, Max admitted that he had a record. He figured I'd find out anyway, with his fingerprints on file. Mrs. Elliot doesn't know about it, and Max said he didn't want her to find out. She's sure going to find out now."

"Thanks to us," Trixie moaned.

"I'd have caught up with him sooner or later," Molinson said. "You do realize that you'll probably have to testify against him?"

Trixie was crushed. "I couldn't."

"Me, either," Honey said.

"If it goes to trial, you'll have no choice," Molinson said. He glanced sidelong at Trixie. "It's part of the 'job,' Miss Detective," he said. He glanced at his watch. "I'd better get up to the Elliots' to wait for Max to get back. I don't know if I should say thank you or not." He headed for his car. "If I were you, I'd get out of those smelly clothes," he said over his shoulder as he got into the car.

Trixie was miserable for the rest of that day and the next. Listlessly she did her chores in the house and garden. She took care of Bobby and tried to share his enthusiasm for whatever they were doing, but she wasn't very successful.

At the moment, they were playing checkers, but Trixie's mind wasn't on the game. She had lost three times in a row. A tear slipped down her cheek.

Bobby misunderstood. "Don't cry, Trixie. You'll win next time. I'll let you," he said sympathetically.

Mrs. Belden overheard. "Bobby, you find something to do by yourself now." She waited until he was out of the room. "Trixie?" she asked, putting her arm gently around Trixie's shoulders.

"Oh, Moms, I've made such a mess of everything!"

"Trixie, you can't blame yourself. You had good intentions, but things turned out badly because of what other people had done."

"But I should have minded my own business, like you and Dad wanted me to," Trixie moaned. "If I hadn't tried to help Mrs. Elliot—"

"Things might have been worse for her if you hadn't become involved. Of course it's a blow to her, finding out about Max's police record. But that's not your fault, either. It would have come out sooner or later. You did accomplish something good," Mrs. Belden said.

Trixie wiped away a tear. "What?" she asked.

Mrs. Belden spread open yesterday's White Plains newspaper to a page of color photographs. One of them was a picture Mart had taken of Mrs. Elliot's sweet pea vines climbing on the umbrella frame.

Trixie stared at the photo. "Well, at least that's something," she murmured. "Not much, but something."

"Trixie," her mother chided. "Not long ago, you were positive this photo was going to win the big grand prize at the end of the contest. Let's have some of that enthusiasm back."

Trixie shrugged. "It's gone, Moms. I'm not so

sure now that Honey and I should even plan on being detectives. I don't want to create problems for people."

"You mustn't feel like that, Trixie," Mrs. Belden said with a sigh. She glanced at the photo, then looked closer. "Why, look! The flowers on this short vine look yellow. I don't recall ever seeing a yellow sweet pea blossom. Were there really yellow flowers when the photo was taken, or is something wrong with the printing here?"

Trixie glanced at the photo without her usual keen interest. "I don't remember. Maybe Mart knows."

Mart came in at that moment. "What do I know?" he asked. "I thought I was supposed to be just a dumb brother."

"I've probably been wrong about that, too," Trixie murmured.

Mart stared at her in disbelief. For once, no big words came to mind. Outside, a car door slammed. Mr. Belden was home from the bank for lunch.

"What's new in town?" Mrs. Belden inquired. "Anything that would perk up this family? The young people are so down in the mouth they're about to trip over their chins."

"I know just how they feel," Peter Belden said, "because right now, I'm feeling the same way."

"Peter! It's hard enough trying to cheer them up. What's wrong with you?"

Trixie's father slumped in a chair. "It's bank business, of course, and I shouldn't say anything. But I had an inquiry from the local Social Security office this morning. They had information that Mrs. Elliot was earning too much money. People with a large, steady income aren't eligible to collect Social Security benefits until they're seventy-two years old."

Mrs. Belden sounded puzzled. "Ethel is under seventy-two, but she certainly isn't earning much money."

"According to the Social Security office, she *has* been," Trixie's father said. "They claim they have proof."

"There must be some mistake," Trixie said in disbelief.

Her father shrugged his shoulders. "I tried

to tell them they were wrong. Ethel certainly hasn't been depositing large sums of money in the bank. The office thinks that she's banking it somewhere else or hiding it. Anyway, they're going to stop sending her Social Security checks. She'll either have to repay what they claim she's received, or they'll hold any more payments."

Trixie was on her feet. "Daddy, you've got to stop them! If you don't, Mrs. Elliot will have to sell her property."

"I argued with them all I could," Peter Belden said wearily. "They didn't go into details with me, but they said that they've seen receipts that show she's been getting much more for her flowers than what she's reported."

Trixie frowned. A familiar light was starting to show in her eyes. "As far as I know, she's been selling her flowers to only one shop."

Mart nodded. "Manton's, in White Plains. Finlay's place."

"I'm sure Ethel wouldn't file false reports with Social Security," Mrs. Belden said. "It must be a mistake. I'm sure that their office will realize that."

183

"Not if Finlay is still up to something," Trixie declared. "And I'm sure he is."

"Is he still in the picture?" Peter Belden asked. "What about Max? He confessed to everything this morning."

"That's impossible!" Trixie gasped. "He couldn't confess to everything. I *know* that Finlay—"

"Max didn't incriminate anyone but himself," Peter Belden interrupted. "One of Molinson's deputies told me this morning. Max took the blame for everything that's happened at Mrs. Elliot's place."

"How could he?" Trixie demanded. "We saw Max in the cornfield while somebody else tried to burn Mrs. Elliot's shed. Max couldn't take the blame for that without involving someone else."

"I remember you telling me about that," agreed her father. "I mentioned it to the deputy. He said Max claimed you were excited and imagined you saw another man trying to set the fire."

"That's not so!" Trixie said.

Mart shook his head. "Will Max go to jail?"

"Not unless his stepmother presses charges," Peter Belden said. "But she doesn't even know he confessed. And I don't think Molinson is going to tell her."

"What about the marijuana?" Trixie asked.

"It's up to Molinson to press charges on that," her father said. "But he can't *prove* that Max planted it. And it was destroyed, anyway. Max said he burned it because he was afraid it would be discovered before he could harvest it."

"I don't believe one word of Max's confession," Trixie said vehemently, her eyes flashing.

Mrs. Belden looked alarmed. "Trixie. . . ."

"Mart," Trixie ordered, "find Brian. We'll need him to drive. If you can't find him, then phone Jim to stand by."

"Trixie!" Mrs. Belden repeated. "Where do you think you're going? There's nothing you can do about any of this. Mrs. Elliot has some sort of mix-up with the government. And Max has confessed to the other crimes. It's all over, as far as you're concerned."

"Unless we do something," Trixie said, "it'll

be all over for Mrs. Elliot. She won't have anything!"

"Trixie," her father spoke seriously. "You have gone as far as you can go on this one. Drop it."

"I can't," Trixie moaned. "I don't believe Max's confession, and I'm sure you don't, either. And I think I know why he did it."

"Why?" her father asked.

"It must have something to do with his father," Trixie said.

"What?" Peter Belden prompted.

"I don't know," Trixie admitted.

Her parents exchanged glances.

"But I know someone who does," Trixie went on. "Mr. Hartman. I'm sure he knows something about Max's father that could clear this all up."

Her mother looked skeptical. "Sam Elliot has been dead for five years," she said.

"But Mr. Hartman knows something about him . . . something that he wouldn't tell us before. Maybe he'll tell us now, to help Mrs. Elliot. Please," Trixie pleaded, "let me go talk to him. He and Mrs. Hartman are Mrs. Elliot's best friends. I know they can help."

Mrs. Belden sighed. "I suppose you're too excited for lunch now, anyway."

Trixie hugged her. "Oh, thank you, Moms!"

Peter Belden raised his eyebrows. "I didn't hear her actually *say* that you could go to the Hartmans'."

Trixie flushed.

"But go ahead," her father said indulgently. "Don't make pests of yourselves, though."

Brian drove Trixie and Mart to the Hartmans' in his jalopy. "Runs like a dream since Tom tuned it up," he said.

"Too bad this case isn't running as smoothly," Mart mumbled.

The Hartmans were in their backyard when the young people arrived. Mr. Hartman was digging in the garden while his wife supervised. After friendly greetings, Mrs. Hartman began pointing out unusual plants in her herb garden. While Brian and Mart listened, Trixie motioned Mr. Hartman aside.

"Well, Trixie," he said, wiping his hands on a handkerchief, "what's on your mind?"

"I'm worried about Mrs. Elliot," Trixie said. "Max might end up going to jail for something he didn't do. That would leave her without anyone."

Hartman scowled. "Molinson told me about the marijuana. I don't think he'll press charges."

"Oh, good!" Trixie exclaimed. "At least Max won't go to jail. I just hope that his being around won't cause more problems for Mrs. Elliot."

Hartman looked puzzled. "First you sound glad that he's not in jail, then you talk as though he belongs there."

"I don't mean that," Trixie said. "I think Max knows what's going on. I think he's been trying to prevent it and not succeeding." Trixie hesitated. "But I thought if you . . . could get him to tell what he knows. . . ."

Mr. Hartman shook his head. "He's had plenty of opportunity to talk. He says there isn't anything to talk about. He's taking all the blame for everything."

188

"I can't believe it," Trixie declared. "I think there's something he doesn't want Mrs. Elliot to know—I don't mean about himself, but about his father, Sam Elliot."

Hartman started to shake his head again. Trixie spoke quickly. "When I was here another time, Mr. Hartman, you hinted something about Sam Elliot—"

"Just a slip of the tongue. I told you then: Sam Elliot is gone, and everything with him. So forget it. Don't disturb Ethel's memories of him."

"Is it more important that she has good memories or that she saves her farm?" Trixie asked. "Because she's going to lose her farm. Max has taken the blame," Trixie declared, "but he can't be responsible. He must know who is but doesn't dare point a finger at that person. The other person must be threatening him with something."

Charles Hartman neither agreed with nor denied that. "And just what do you think Sam Elliot has to do with it?"

"I don't know," Trixie admitted in puzzled

frustration. "But I'm positive who the other person is. It's Al Finlay. Under the name of Manton, he runs a flower shop in White Plains. He wants Mrs. Elliot's property for some reason. He's been doing all those things to ruin her business. Now he's almost forced Mrs. Elliot to sell her property by having her Social Security payments stopped."

"What?" Hartman asked, frowning. "Who told you that?"

Trixie swallowed. "My father. But I'm not supposed to say anything—"

"I understand," Hartman said.

"I think Finlay lied about how much money he's paid Mrs. Elliot for her flowers," Trixie went on. "And now they're going to stop her Social Security payments."

Hartman shook his head slowly. After a moment, he spoke over his shoulder to the others. "Anyone want some cold soda? Trixie and I will bring some out." He nodded toward the house, and Trixie followed him inside.

In the living room, Hartman telephoned information to get the number of Manton's Flower Shop in White Plains. Then he dialed that number. "Hello?" he said. "This is Mr. Wilson of the Social Security Administration. Is Mr. Manton in? . . . He's not? . . . Well, perhaps you could answer a few questions for me, miss."

Trixie leaned close to try to overhear. When Hartman finally hung up after several minutes, his expression was thoughtful. "That was lucky. She didn't know about the investigation. But she *did* know that Manton pays Ethel in cash for her flowers—twenty or thirty dollars at a time, usually. In the ledger, though, a zero has been added to make it look like she'd been paid two or three *hundred* dollars."

"That explains it!" Trixie exclaimed. "Manton—I mean Finlay—probably made a complaint to the Social Security office. They looked at his books, then compared his figures to Mrs. Elliot's reports of her earnings."

"Since he paid in cash," Hartman muttered, "it really comes down to his word against hers." He looked squarely at Trixie. "All right, young lady. I'll talk to Max later today. I don't know if it'll make any difference, but I'll do it."

"Oh, thank you, Mr. Wil—uh, Mr. Hartman," Trixie said.

Hartman pointed a finger at her. "Forget you ever heard that little tactic," he advised.

"Yes, sir!" Trixie said, smiling.

The Unseen Treasure · 11

BRIAN BACKED HIS JALOPY down the Hartman driveway and onto Glen Road. Trixie was telling him and Mart about what Mr. Hartman had done. "So he said he'd talk to Max," she concluded. "Maybe he'll find a new lead for us to follow."

Brian eyed the gas gauge. "We won't be following anything if I don't get some gas," he said.

"Drop me off at Mrs. Elliot's on the way,"

Trixie instructed her brother.

"Hey!" Mart said. "You just said that Mr. Hartman was going to talk to Max."

"I want to talk to Mrs. Elliot," Trixie explained, "about those yellow sweet peas. Moms didn't think there was such a thing."

"Okay," Brian said, pulling to the side of the road at Mrs. Elliot's drive. "We'll come back for you after I fill 'er up."

Trixie walked up the drive and knocked on Mrs. Elliot's door. Mrs. Elliot answered, wearing an apron and holding a beautiful fresh corsage.

"Why, hello, Trixie. Do come in," she said cheerfully.

She doesn't know about the Social Security payments yet, Trixie thought with a twinge. "Hello," she said as cheerily as she could. "Brian dropped me off. I wanted to ask you something." She eyed the corsage in Mrs. Elliot's hand. "Can I help?" she asked.

"Well, if you wouldn't mind," Mrs. Elliot said, "you could help me with some corsages for a reception this afternoon."

194

"Lead me to them," Trixie said, glad to have an excuse for staying.

"I thought I had plenty of time to get them finished without Max's help. He's working in the barn," Mrs. Elliot said. "But then a man phoned and talked for quite a while. He wants to see me this afternoon."

"A man from the realty company?" Trixie inquired.

"No, that man hasn't called again, and I can't find his firm listed anywhere in the phone book."

Trixie wondered if Manton himself had posed as a realtor, disguising his voice. Perhaps he had had someone else pose as a realtor.

Mrs. Elliot went on. "The man who called today is from a company that raises and sells flower seeds. He saw the photograph you entered for me in the newspaper contest. He tried to telephone me yesterday, when it was printed in the paper, but I was in White Plains."

Trixie nodded, remembering hearing the ringing telephone.

"He wanted to know about the yellow sweet

peas that appeared in the photograph. He said no seed company has ever been able to produce yellow sweet peas." Mrs. Elliot looked bewildered. "I had to admit that I'd never heard of yellow sweet peas, either."

"They're growing right here in your garden!" Trixie exclaimed. "That's what I came to ask about."

"They're right in plain sight," Mrs. Elliot said with a chuckle, "but somehow I just didn't notice them. The man from the seed company wanted to know if there was a mistake in the picture."

"That's just exactly what Moms said!" Trixie recalled.

"I told him there really are yellow flowers," Mrs. Elliot continued. "He indicated that the vines could be worth a great deal of money to me."

"How wonderful!" Trixie said happily. "But please go slow, Mrs. Elliot. Don't accept his offer too fast, and don't let him dig up the vine or have you sign any papers until you've talked to a lawyer."

Trixie helped select blossoms from several bunches of flowers on a table. Mrs. Elliot snipped off the stems and added them to corsages. "Where did the yellow flowers come from?" Trixie asked.

Mrs. Elliot shook her head. "Sam, my late husband, was a genius with plants. He was always experimenting and keeping notes. Early this spring, while cleaning out part of the barn, I found a jarful of seeds he had labeled 'Sweet Peas, Special.' I planted them with my other sweet pea seeds, thinking they were just a hardier variety of the usual colors."

"But now," Trixie said, "we know what he meant by 'Special.' He must have kept records about their development. Did you find any records?"

"I didn't look for anything like that," Mrs. Elliot replied. "They wouldn't be of use to me— I don't have Sam's know-how about cross-breeding plants and such."

"Where did he keep the records?" Trixie asked.

Mrs. Elliot raised her eyebrows. "I found the

deed to the property and some fire and car insurance papers in his desk. When I had what was needed, I had his desk and the records about his plants moved out to the barn. Having them in here just reminded me too painfully of. . . ."

Trixie nodded understandingly. She tried to hold down her excitement. "Mrs. Elliot, if records can be found to verify the new variety, it would be even more valuable. We should go out to the barn and look for them before the man from the seed company gets here."

Mrs. Elliot nodded, then looked at the table of flowers and corsages. "Oh, dear, I've got to get those finished first. You go ahead, Trixie. Sam's plant records are in a ring binder with a hard green cover. It should be in the bottom drawer of the desk. If you can't find it, I'll be out shortly to help."

"I'll find it," Trixie said. She dashed out to the barn. After searching among a clutter of old furniture and boxes, she hauled back a sheet and sneezed in the dust cloud that arose. The desk was underneath. After moving some cartons, Trixie pulled out the bottom drawer and lifted out the binder.

She found pages headed by the common and Latin names of flowers, followed by dates and notations on planting, seeds, and blossoms. Trixie flipped through the pages, looking for something about sweet peas, but there was nothing.

She groaned. Maybe Sam Elliot had made his notations under a Latin name. What on earth would that be? Mrs. Elliot might know it or have a book where it could be looked up.

As Trixie picked up the binder, a long white envelope slipped out. Picking it up, she saw writing on one side of it. She gaped at what she read: "To be opened after my death. Sam Elliot."

Below that was another line, underlined for emphasis: "Not to be opened in the presence of my wife."

Trixie stared at the sealed flap. What should she do now? She couldn't take this to Mrs. Elliot. Should she take it to her father or Mr. Hartman? She read Sam Elliot's writing again.

He hadn't specified *who* was to open this, just that it wasn't to be done in his wife's presence.

With trembling fingers, Trixie opened the envelope. She withdrew several folded pages. The first page was a short, handwritten note.

I do not want Ethel to know about some of the matters contained here. That is why I have not placed this with other papers needed for the settlement of my estate. I'm requesting that whoever finds this will see that Ethel gains from the legacy enclosed. But please do not reveal to her the other information herein.

The next page was a loose-leaf sheet removed from the ring binder. It was headed "Sweet Peas (very good possibility for a new and valuable yellow variety)."

It's no longer just a possibility, Trixie thought.

The remaining pages also contained notes about some kind of plants, and also dates and large amounts of money written in. There was another handwritten note with these pages. As Trixie began reading this note, her face paled and her mouth dropped open.

Suddenly Trixie was aware of voices. Max

and Mr. Hartman. They were somewhere near-by in the barn, and it sounded as if they were arguing.

Trixie's attention returned to Sam Elliot's writing. She could hardly believe what she was reading, but it was there in black and white, in Sam Elliot's own words. As she finished, she again became aware of the rising voices of Max and Mr. Hartman.

"Listen to me, Max," Charles Hartman was saying. "Trixie Belden knows, and now I also know, that you've been trying to protect Ethel from Al Finlay, alias Manton. But you've been failing. Now he's managed to stop her Social Security payments!"

Trixie strained to hear. She couldn't see the two men, so she assumed that they could not see her. For a moment, she heard only the buzz-ing of a fly.

Then Max spoke, resignedly. "I'll tell you this much. When I first ran away to the city, well, it was tough going. I managed to get by with odd jobs here and there. Then I made some so-called friends. Before I knew it, I was mixed up in a robbery. We got caught. That's the police record I told Sergeant Molinson about. When I got out of jail, I'd had enough of the city. I came back here. My father was dead, and my stepmother needed my help here."

Max paused, then went on. "Everything was fine until early this spring. Then Al Finlay came to see me. He'd heard about me from one of my cell mates. He wanted me to get possession of this place and grow marijuana and other drugs for him. I told him *no*. The place wasn't mine. That's why I didn't want any part of ownership when Ethel offered it to me.

"But that didn't stop Finlay. He was determined to get this place. I warned him that if anything happened to my stepmother, I'd tell the police everything I knew about him, which is plenty.

"So Finlay began trying to force her to sell out. He would have stolen her Social Security checks if I hadn't told her to send them to the bank. He beat me on the water pump, though. And somehow he managed to plant marijuana in the cornfield—probably while we were out delivering flowers.

"But he won't be able to prove those phony high payments for her flowers. Ethel doesn't begin to grow nearly enough flowers to bring that much money. As soon as the Social Security office checks other flower shops for the going rate on flowers she does raise, they'll know Finlay's lying. They won't stop her checks."

"Keep talking," Hartman said.

"That's all there is," Max mumbled.

"No, there's more," Hartman insisted. "If it were only what you've told me, you could have gone to the police to protect Ethel. But you couldn't, because Finlay is holding something over you."

"My police record," Max said.

"Hogwash," Hartman snapped. "You paid your penalty on that score. You also told Molinson about it. Finlay's threatening to reveal something about your father, isn't he? Something you don't want Ethel to know about." It was more a statement than a question.

Max's voice flared back. "Leave things as

they are! Ethel's going to be okay now. There's nothing more to talk about."

Trixie heard sounds of movement, as though Max were going to leave the barn. "Wait!" she yelled. "I've got something to show you!"

She hurried through the cool darkness to the other side of the barn. Mr. Hartman and Max scowled at her.

"I—I wasn't listening in on purpose," Trixie explained. "Mrs. Elliot sent me to the barn to look for something in Mr. Elliot's old desk. I overheard you talking." She waved the papers. "I've found the answer to what's been going on around here!"

She handed the empty envelope to Hartman, who read the words and passed it to Max.

"Let me see those papers," Hartman said.

Trixie handed them to him and turned to face Max. "Your father knew you ran away to the city because you discovered that he was raising and selling drugs—marijuana and heroin poppies—to Al Finlay."

Max clenched his hands. "I wanted no part of that dirty business, but Finlay was trying to blackmail me into growing some marijuana on this property."

Trixie gestured to the pages Hartman was reading. "Your father's conscience bothered him after you left. He destroyed everything that had any connection with drugs. All the money he'd made from them he donated anonymously to a drug rehabilitation center in the city. That's why there was no money in his estate when he died shortly after that. He'd wanted to let you know that he'd reformed—that he was sorry—but he couldn't find you."

Charles Hartman looked up from the confession he was reading. "This explains a lot to me. I suspected what Sam was doing and why Max ran away. Sam was afraid that Finlay might try to make trouble for you or Ethel, so he kept very careful records. There's enough here to send Finlay to prison for the rest of his life. I'll give these to Sergeant Molinson personally, and I'll make sure that Ethel never knows about it. Finlay's got nothing on you now, Max," Mr. Hartman assured him. Turning to Trixie, he asked, "What's the 'legacy' Sam mentions?"

Trixie explained about the yellow sweet peas Sam Elliot had developed. "They're worth a lot of money," she said. "The man from the seed company will be here any time. I'd better tell Mrs. Elliot that I found the records about the yellow sweet peas."

Charles Hartman grasped her arm. "Don't give any hint about what else you found."

"Never," Trixie promised.

Trixie hurried up the back steps and into the cottage. "I found the records," she called. "They were right where you said—"

Mrs. Elliot was not in the living room. The front door was slightly ajar, and Trixie could hear Mrs. Elliot's voice from the front porch.

". . . kind of you," she was saying, "but it won't be necessary for me to sell the property now. I've just discovered that my late husband developed a new variety of sweet pea that's very valuable. A seed company is going to buy the rights to them."

Trixie wondered who was out there—it obviously wasn't the man from the seed company.

"I'd like to see those sweet peas," the voice

of Al Finlay—known to Mrs. Elliot only as Manton, the owner of a flower shop—said smoothly. "Show them to me."

"No!" Trixie screamed. She burst through the doorway and onto the porch. "Don't do it, Mrs. Elliot! He'll destroy them. He *wants* you to have to sell this place—to him. He's the one who's been trying to make you sell!"

Al Finlay stared. "You!" he said. His gaze darted past her. Mr. Hartman and Max were running from the barn in response to her scream.

Al Finlay grabbed Trixie roughly and yanked her toward him. He pulled a gun. "Keep away!" he shouted to Mr. Hartman and Max. "You, too," he told Mrs. Elliot, who cowered in fear. He clutched Trixie in front of him with one strong arm.

"Finlay," Mr. Hartman called. "It's all over. Drop the gun!"

"Forget it, old man!" Finlay growled. "I've got the meddlesome girl!" Dragging Trixie along, he stepped backward toward the porch steps. "Don't anybody try anything," he warned.

At that moment, Brian's old jalopy pulled into the driveway, wheezed once, and shot a loud backfire. Apparently it was running "normally" again. Finlay jumped, releasing Trixie and stumbling backward down the steps. His gun clattered to the walk. Hartman was on him in an instant, holding him in an armlock.

"Don't try to squirm out of it," Brian said knowledgeably.

"Call the police, Ethel," Mr. Hartman advised, firmly gripping the angry Finlay.

Mr. Hartman and Max accompanied Sergeant Molinson when he took the prisoner into town. The Beldens remained briefly to help calm Mrs. Elliot.

"I don't understand it," Mrs. Elliot said. "Mr. Manton always seemed like such a nice man."

"His name wasn't Manton," Trixie told her. "And he won't be causing any more trouble for you. I know."

Just then, a taxi pulled up, and a man in a suit with a carnation in the lapel climbed out. "Mrs. Elliot?" he asked. "I spoke to you this morning about a new variety of yellow sweet peas. . . ."

That night, all of the Bob-Whites were invited to Crabapple Farm for dinner so Trixie could tell them about everything that had happened. She told about finding the papers in the old desk but not, of course, about Sam Elliot's confession. That would be her secret, forever.

"The 'hidden treasure' was never actually hidden at all. It's just that no one ever really *saw* it for what it was. It was right there in front of us the whole time," Trixie concluded. "Those yellow sweet peas are going to be worth a lot of money for Mrs. Elliot."

"Ahem!" Mart sat up straight and stretched his neck, as if expecting to hear something.

"Thanks to Mart's photograph," Trixie acknowledged. "If it wasn't for that, we might never have known."

"Thank you." Mart bowed grandly. "Well," he said, glancing around with a twinkle in his eyes, "I guess this wraps up another case for our illustrious sibling sleuth. Right, Trixie?" He winked broadly at his sister.

Trixie smiled, hoping she'd remember the words he'd told her to say. "That's right," she said. "I think I'll call this one 'The Case of the Leguminous Legacy.'"

Mart beamed. Everyone else groaned.

T